Yet to be Determined

T.R. Baker

Copyright © 2017 by T.R. Baker

All rights reserved. Printed in the United States of America. No part of this book may be used or reproduced in any manner whatsoever without written permission except in the case of brief quotations embodied in articles and reviews. For information address T. R. Baker, P.O. Box 1342, Decatur, GA 30031.

Cover Photo: Jaylin Jackson
Graphic Design: India Nabarro

Photos reprinted on the cover with permission of Sandy Blake and Gudrun Hughes, Copyright 2017

ISBN-10: 0-9857647-3-2
ISBN-13: 978-0-9857647-3-9
Library of Congress Control Number: 2017901051

Yet to be Determined

Memoriam
Freddie L. "Preacher Man" Hargrove, Sr.
1935-2016
(He would have really loved being mentioned in a book.)

ACKNOWLEDGMENTS

A huge thank you to Maggie Monastesse of Decatur Estate & Way Back Antiques, who did not hesitate to say "yes" when I asked if I could have a few pictures taken in her business for the cover of the book. A big, love-filled thank you to Jaylin Jackson for being a photographer/videographer extraordinaire. I never would have guessed that we'd laugh as hard as we laugh together and that we would always have so much to talk about. I'm looking forward to many more conversations and laughs in the future. A bow of appreciation and thanks to India Nabarro, Georgia State University, Junior Graphic Designer, for designing the cover that spoke loudest to what I saw in my head and felt in my heart.

Research is always a great adventure, so I want to thank all of the resources I used (because I don't want anybody contacting me saying, "that sounds familiar"). So here goes. Thank you to: Wikipedia for information regarding the African Slave Trade, Mali Empire, Mandinka People, Wilberforce University, Howard University, Alzheimer's disease, Brotherhood of Sleeping Car Porters, Neighborhoods of Chicago, and History of African Americans in Chicago; Fulani – Marriage and Family (www.everyculture.com); *Top 10 Dessert and Ice Wines* (Stacy Slinkard); Culinary School.org; *Words for Your Enjoyment: Wife Beaters*

(Paul Davidson); *Encyclopedia of the Harlem Renaissance* (Aberjhani and Sandra L. West); *Wedding Day* (Gwendolyn Bennett); *The Harlem Renaissance* (Steven Watson); and *The Rise and Fall of Jim Crow, The Great Depression* (Richard Wormser).

Thank you to Audrey Horn for the times you gave me the motivation I needed to move forward with the story, even though it still took me far too long to finish it. Love, hugs, and thank you to Cindy K. who not only read the manuscript, but wrote notes and edited where needed then insisted that we sit down to discuss what she had read. Our conversations gave me life and encouraged me to want to write more. Pamela Williams, thank you for asking, often, "Are you finished with the book yet?" You kept me artistically obligated to finish what I had started. Our conversations are also a tremendous source of comfort. You know what I know and you feel what I feel. And a big old thank you to everyone that continues to encourage me to write.

Most importantly, thank you to Jehovah God for blessing me with the gift to do something positive with the written word. (James 1:17) I hope that what I write is not only a source of entertainment, but that it somehow motivates others in whatever way they need to be motivated.

Prologue

It seemed like the three of them had been together forever – sisters of fortune, three of a kind. Their ages were now 78, 75, and, of course, the baby, Miss Alaina, at 73. She was the most outspoken; the most garish of them all. Her mouth was pretty filthy for an older woman, but even with that there was a lively, entertaining ring to her voice. Though the three of them together were what most would refer to as eccentric, the oldest of the three was very tight-fisted and authoritative. The middle sister was reserved and proper, and the third sister, with her bracelets from her wrist midway up her forearm, was straight Bohemian. All of them were still striking beauties and in their day, according to them, could have had men from one end of the United States to the other. I got the impression that each one of them was independent and strong in their own way.

The Roberts sisters were products of parents of the Harlem Renaissance. They had witnessed countless parties, numerous jazz sets, and who knows what else. Even at their current ages, they were artists that produced work that exuded racial consciousness. They were products of a time that produced aristocratic, stately, artistic Negros. The three had found themselves in the presence of Langston Hughes, Jessie Redmon Faust, Zora Neale Hurston, Duke Ellington, Count Basie, Bessie Smith and countless other writers, poets, and musical geniuses, the likes of which have not been duplicated. Even though all three of the ladies were too young to completely appreciate the significance of their experiences, they seemed to have reaped the benefits of their associations.

As we spoke, each one of them referred to the other as "sister," which initially made it very difficult for me to keep up with the conversation. On occasion, they called each other by name or by special nicknames, which only they used, and when they did this, it was almost melodic. Their voices often harmoniously intertwined, as if they had practiced all their lives to speak in tandem.

I came to know the sisters because of Miss Claudette's book, "The Emancipation Continuum of the Negro in America." She argued that in the '80s, even after the Harlem Renaissance of the 1920s and '30s, the stock market drop of the '40s, the Civil Rights Movement of the 1960s, and the Black Power movement of the '70s, Blacks were still struggling for emancipation to a position of social, racial, and economic equality, even though modern society could not otherwise function without the advent of the countless contributions they had so graciously bestowed upon America.

When I met the three sisters in the late '90s, it was long past the Black Power movement that had catered to a strong sense of racial pride, the creation of black political and cultural institutions that nurtured and promoted black collective interests, advanced black values, and secured black autonomy – another, yet, socially enlightening era for Blacks. Even amidst their struggles, as always, Blacks still managed to somehow find a happy medium in their communities. The residuals of the "free love" movement of the '60s, accentuated by, seemingly, endless amounts of weed, which, by the way, one of the sisters still partook of on a regular basis, didn't hurt to keep some things moving in the '70s.

Miss Claudette's book made it clear that many of the characteristics of Blacks, particularly those that exhibited a non-defeatist attitude, were intrinsic of the indigenous people of Africa that we once were. In addition to anything that I might have mentioned about her previously, she was also extremely unapologetically Afrocentric.

My story actually began in 1998 when I ran across Claudette Roberts' book in the library on the campus of Miles College in Birmingham, Alabama. One of our major, junior class assignments for the semester was to choose any person from the Harlem Renaissance and share the significance of this person, as well as show how he/she was influenced by the era, and then be prepared to discuss it from our journal of research that we had to keep our notes in. When I first saw the assignment, it seemed ridiculous that any professor would give me a project that would, obviously, last almost an entire semester and possibly interfere with my other class assignments. So, I went to the library early in the semester in search of a book about the Harlem Renaissance that was not the "typical" historical perspective of that period of time. I wanted a personal story, something that sounded almost fictional in nature, something that encapsulated the excitement and glitter of the time and, according to my best guess, Claudette Roberts and her sisters experienced the Harlem Renaissance, as well as the Civil Rights Movement of the 1960s. Though Ms. Claudette's book did not directly address the Harlem Renaissance, she and her sisters did experience it firsthand, so her book was going to be the book that I worked from.

When I stumbled across her book, the jacket indicated she was a local author. Well, local as in she lived in Jemison, Alabama, in between Birmingham and Montgomery. I could easily make that drive one weekend. I did a little further research and found that her two sisters, that she acknowledged in her book, also lived there and were equally accomplished in their own rights. Every newspaper and magazine article I found was more flattering than the last. Being the overachiever that I am, I reasoned that a personal interview with the author and her sisters would give me an edge over the other students in my class and result in an A+ that would, more than likely, throw my grade right off the chart.

It was very easy to find Claudette Roberts. Actually, once I arrived in Jemison, it was easy enough to confirm that she lived there, but the citizens of Jemison were very protective of her and her two sisters, who, I was going to quickly learn, were renaissance mavericks. They were local celebrities, of sort, and I couldn't get anyone to give me directions to their house. I was, instead, directed to the sheriff's office. It wasn't hard to find because downtown consisted of a short, one block, row of buildings. It was next to the fire department at the end of the block, across the street from where I stood.

As I took my time walking down the street, I returned waves to the few cars that passed by that, I'm sure, recognized me as a stranger in town, but waved nonetheless. Once I reached the small brick building that was used as the sheriff's office, I opened the door where I was immediately greeted by a very grandmotherly, older, white woman with blonde hair, sitting at a desk to the right in the room. I said hello, introduced myself, and then told her I had been sent there because I was looking for Ms. Claudette Roberts. She asked me to have a seat in one of the three, wooden chairs across from her desk, up against the wall behind me. I turned to sit down as the grandmotherly lady got up and walked into an office located in the corner of the room behind her desk.

She soon returned smiling. "Miss Shae, Sheriff

Granger will see you now."

I thanked her and walked across the room to the sheriff's office. As I entered his office, he walked around his desk and extended his hand. He was taller than I expected and really good looking for an older, white guy. His skin was tan and he looked like he worked out. I was looking at him so hard that I almost missed being asked to take a seat. From that point on, he grilled me like I was on the FBI's Ten Most Wanted Fugitive list.

ONE

"I promise, Sheriff Granger, I'm a student at Miles College in Birmingham. I can show you my ID."

"Anybody can make an ID. What's your name and why'd you say you were looking for Miss Claudette Roberts, again?"

"My name is Shae Leslie. I'm a junior in college and one of our class assignments is to do a project about the Harlem Renaissance and Miss Roberts wrote a book…"

"Ma'am, Miss Roberts has written several books; which one are you talking about?"

"The Emancipation Continuum of the Negro in America."

"Is she expecting you?"

My nerves were starting to get the best of me and I was beginning to think that I wasn't going to see the Roberts sisters after all, ever.

"No, sir, I called information to get her telephone number, but it was unlisted and I didn't want to write her a letter and wait for a response because that was going to take too long. I thought if I drove down today I could find her house and, maybe, stop by and at least meet her and schedule time to see her another day, if she's too busy to talk to me today," I rambled, teary-eyed.

The sheriff sat down at his desk and made a phone call. After hanging up the phone, he came around his desk and walked over to me, and asked me to follow him. Once we were outside he directed me to his car.

"Get in on the other side. I'm going to take you to see Miss Roberts. She'll call me when you're finished and I'll come back to get you."

Initially, the ride was quiet and uncomfortable, as calls echoed from the sheriff's radio. I guess he felt the tension and couldn't take it anymore either.

He glared at me. "Now look here. You better not do anything with that school project of yours to embarrass these ladies. Do you understand?"

I nodded my head affirmatively.

"Miss Claudette and her sisters don't bother anybody; they mind their business; they're real ladies."

"Yes, sir, I understand."

He turned away and looked back at the road. We'd taken the main road back out of Jemison and were now on an old highway. As we turned onto a dirt road, I noticed the beautiful flowers on both sides. I made a mental note to ask the sisters if they planted them. Eventually, we turned down a long, narrow road lined with old, oak trees sprinkled with Spanish moss. The trees opened up to a meticulously, landscaped yard that might have been just shy of being called Paradise. Situated perfectly amid it was a big, beautiful, old, white house with tall, red double-doors and black shutters. The long drive became a circular drive that pulled right up to the stairs of a wraparound porch.

As if on cue, the red doors dramatically opened to reveal three beautiful, older women who sauntered out onto the front porch, as if they were presenting themselves to the paparazzi. One sister, wearing a multi-color dashiki over a khaki wrap-skirt, had her silver-grey hair wrapped in a beautiful head scarf; the second sister had on wide-legged dark blue jeans, a crisp white blouse with French cuffs, a pearl necklace with matching pearl earrings, and snow white canvas tennis shoes; and the last sister wore a long, denim skirt with a multi-colored crochet vest over a brown camisole.

At first glance, I didn't know why, but I knew it was going to be an experience of a lifetime. Sheriff Granger had gotten out of the car and was opening my car door. I stepped out, not knowing whether I should smile, curtsy, or what. The sheriff, knowing the sisters as he did, exercised etiquette and common sense, something that eluded me at that moment.

"Good afternoon, ladies. I'd like you to meet Miss Shae Leslie. She's visiting Jemison from Miles College in Birmingham."

I didn't know what to say because the sisters had yet to acknowledge me. "Good afternoon. I'd be honored if I could sit down with all of you and tell you why I'm here today."

I could tell I was being thoroughly checked out from head to toe. Sheriff Granger had already gotten the okay to bring me, so he was comfortable with leaving me with the sisters.

"Well, ladies, I think my business here is done. I'll look for a call when y'all are finished visiting."

Smiling, Miss Claudette finally spoke. "Thank you, Sheriff Granger. It was very kind of you to escort Miss Shae to our home. We'll certainly give you a call when we're ready for you to return for her. Actually, if you'd like to stay and have lunch, you know you're more than welcome to join us."

"Miss Claudette, it would be my pleasure, but I better get back to town, maybe another time."

"Of course…"

It was quite evident that the sheriff was attracted to Miss Claudette and I wasn't too sure that she wasn't attracted to him, as well.

Obviously bored with the scene, Miss Alaina broke the monotony. "Young lady, please, come in. Sister, see Sheriff Granger off and we'll be waiting for you in the dining room."

Miss Claudette walked down the stairs to see the sheriff off as Miss Zora and Miss Alaina escorted me into their home.

TWO

The Roberts' home was spotless. Everywhere I looked there were antiques – the kind that you see in magazines or museums. It must have taken them years to collect all that they had acquired, which, by the way, looked like it had come from all over the world. After being led to a bathroom to, not only wash my hands, but to freshen up, we had lunch in the formal dining room at a table fit for a queen. Lunch was served on gold trimmed, white plates with a pink, yellow, and blue flower design. I wasn't sure but the dishes appeared to me to be really fine china. I was too afraid to ask.

I got the impression that I would have been scolded and told that it was ill-mannered to make that kind of inquiry at the table. During lunch, most of the conversation was about me. The sisters wanted to find out where I was from; how old I was; where my parents were; if they were still alive; if I had siblings, and how many. By the time we finished eating our puff pastry stuffed with chicken and salad, fresh from their garden, we settled in the parlor with a pot of hot, herbal tea. I think, by the end of lunch they were convinced that I was there for a sincere purpose.

I followed as Miss Claudette and Miss Alaina led me to the parlor, which was a room off to the right of the living room – I had never seen a parlor before. There were wall to wall, floor to ceiling windows and the room was filled with sunshine and every green plant imaginable. It looked like what I'd expect a parlor to look like – comfortable. It then occurred to me, I had left my questions in my car. I would have to wing it. Fortunately, I had my tape recorder in my purse. Miss Alaina sat down and looked at me fancifully.

"So, tell us more about your project, dear. We've been interviewed and such, but I don't know that any of us have ever been a project. I'm sure you'd like to get started." Her smile was warm, welcoming, and mischievous.

"Well, I left my list of questions that I wanted to ask in my car, but, really, I want to discuss what it was like growing up during the Harlem Renaissance. From everything that I've ever read, it seems like it was a great time in history for African Americans."

Waving her hand at me, Miss Alaina chuckled, "I was worried that all you wanted to talk about was that old book Sister wrote. It's just full of facts. And who cares about that, right? You should ask Sister about her life. Sister, tell this young lady about some of the things you've done."

Miss Claudette smiled as she handed me a cup of peppermint tea. In that brief moment I could see in her eyes that she was quickly reminiscing over the many years of her life.

"You shouldn't raise this young lady's hopes like that, Sister. Zora should probably be here to get us started. She's the oldest, you know." She paused. "Well, let's not wake her. She has to have her nap every day after lunch and she really isn't that delightful if you disturb her from her rest. I think we can at least get started without her. She'll join us in about 30 minutes or so."

"Sister, start with Mother and Father," Miss Alaina chimed in.

I turned on my tape recorder as Miss Claudette began.

"Of course, Mother and Father, from the stories that they told us from the early 1900s, both grew up, not necessarily poor. Though, Negroes were still trying to make a way for themselves. Mother's parents were a little more privileged than some Negroes because both Grandmother and Grandfather Butler were mulatto. You're familiar with that term, aren't you?"

I nodded affirmatively.

"Before we go on, Miss Shae, it would be most appreciated if…" She paused. "What I'm trying to say is you're a young lady. So, when you are saying yes, instead of nodding your head, you should actually say yes."

She didn't wait for me to respond before she

continued with her previous line of thought. "Mother told us that Grandmother could actually pass for white, so white folk were really taken with her, especially the men. Because she was so fair-skinned she was only used in the house to care for the children. So, very early in her life she was taught to read and write. As a result of that she also had much finer clothes than most slaves. She was given the young miss's hand me downs, you see. Grandmother also learned how to sing and play the piano, as well. I think that pleased them in the house because, in addition to taking care of the children, she could also entertain guests during dinner parties, something she apparently did often."

"What did your grandmother look like?"

Miss Alaina closed her eyes as she spoke. "From what mother told us, Grandmother was beautiful. She was very stately with long, black hair. She wasn't of short stature, but she wasn't exactly tall either. I guess that would make her of average height. Her eyes were extraordinary; they were naturally dark and alluring. Mother had eyes just like her, so we didn't have to use too much of our imagination to understand what she meant when she described her mother's eyes. Amazingly, in spite of her circumstances, Grandmother had a beautiful personality and a very strong constitution."

I tried to imagine how their grandmother must have looked. I could only envision a beautiful, light-skinned woman with an alarmingly beautiful smile. The Roberts sisters were extremely beautiful themselves, so it wasn't very much of a stretch to consider what their grandmother might have looked like.

Miss Alaina continued. "And Grandfather, he was a handsome man. He grew up on a different plantation. Of course, they didn't meet until after slavery had ended. He also grew up in his master's house. I'm not quite sure what he did, but his master kept him out of the baking sun because of his fair skin. Word was he looked just like his father, the master, and that's why he was really kept out of the field. Well, that, and the fact that he was the only son that the master had. The mistress of the house could only seem to birth girls for him – five of them to be exact. Grandfather grew to be a very tall man with shiny, coal black hair and green eyes. By all accounts, he was a fancy man – as fancy as a Negro could be back in those days.

Well, after slavery ended, Grandmother's father gave her a piece of land on his property. She was, after all, his child. She was a young woman when all of this took place, so apparently she came to the conclusion that she wouldn't have to work in such a servile position in the house anymore after acquiring land. She was also an adventurous girl and there were things out in the world to see and experience, and she needed her own money to do it. She found herself a job in a little dress shop, mostly folding, cleaning, ironing, and occasionally running errands for the lady who owned the shop. That's how she met grandfather, running an errand.

Now, Grandfather had heard things about her, about this beautiful, mulatto, slave girl from one of the other plantations, but he didn't think he'd ever see her, let alone meet her, especially since slavery had ended, even though he also had taken a job in town, as a blacksmith's assistant. One day, as he was taking a short break with some of the other young Negro men, grandmother passed by. She didn't have any experience with men, but Grandfather caught her eye. Even in his work clothes, he shined like a pretty, new penny. He stood up as she walked by. She smiled at him and said hello, and then continued on her way. He found out from the other young men that she was the young lady that all the talk had been about. At that very moment, he set his mind on one day making her his wife.

"So, did they start talking that day or what?" I wanted to know.

Miss Alaina, tiring of Miss Claudette's long version of the story, interrupted. "Damn, Sister, the child is going to wither and die before you get to the good part of the story with Grandmother and Grandfather."

I really wanted to laugh, but, instead, I smiled. I wasn't sure how Miss Claudette was going to react to Miss Alaina's abrupt interruption of her story of their grandparents, which I was quite interested in hearing.

Miss Claudette, being the lady she appeared to be, didn't even acknowledge her sister with more than a sharp glance, which, obviously, meant more than I realized because Miss Alaina waved her hand at her sister, crossed her legs, and sat back in her chair.

Miss Claudette continued. "Grandfather was completely taken with Grandmother the first time he saw her. He was a handsome man, and rather arrogant, so there was no doubt in his mind that Grandmother would accept his advances and soon begin courting him."

"So, I take it, your grandfather was also a smooth talker."

Alaina retorted, "More like a sh—"

"Sister, please!"

It was apparent that Miss Alaina was the fire starter in the family, as well as the one that talked all the mess. But, again, at Miss Claudette's urging, she sat back in her chair. This time more like a spoiled child than an eager listener.

"No more interruptions, Sister. Please."

Miss Zora must have either finished her nap or heard Miss Claudette when she raised her voice to reprimand her sister's frequent interruptions because she appeared at the door with lines across her forehead and a frown on her face. She looked so stern that I thought she was going to suggest that I leave, but instead she commented to both of her sisters.

"Alaina, you know Sister tells a story slower than molasses – that's nothing new. Let her tell the story the way she wants to tell the story. I'm sure the young lady has better things to do than to sit here all day and night just to get information for a class project. And, Sister, you know Alaina is rude and impatient. Try to hurry along, just a little bit, so this young lady can go on."

Neither one of the sisters appeared offended by the fact that Miss Zora came in and took control of the situation. Instead, they both nodded as if the word had been spoken and thoroughly understood.

Miss Zora continued. "Claudette, please, when you get to a good stopping point just let Sister pick up the story from there. I think that way everybody gets to put in her two cents. Is that okay, Sister?" Smiling, she looked at both of them.

Her smile seemed almost uncomfortable. She didn't strike me as someone who smiled a lot. She actually looked rather sad, like a long-lasting, old sadness, from way down, deep inside.

Miss Alaina was the first to respond. "That's all I'm talking about, Sister. I apologize, Claudette. I won't interrupt again."

Miss Claudette, devoid of emotion, one way or the other, graciously accepted her apology and continued with her story right where she had previously left off.

"Now, Grandfather showed up at the store the very next day, to sweep Grandmother off of her feet, but she wasn't having it. It wasn't that she was playing coy; she had never been courted before. Grandfather actually ended up visiting that store every day for almost a week before Grandmother would do little more than smile and wish him a good day. According to Mother, the shopkeeper actually pulled Grandmother to the side one day and told her that Grandfather was sweet on her. We were told that, at first, Grandmother didn't think that was possible. She was a very humble, unassuming, young woman.

By the end of the week Grandmother was taken with Grandfather's persistence and she accepted his offer to have a cold drink one day after work. They were married about three months later – and about a little over nine months after that Lily Rose, our mother, was born."

"So, your mother was an only child?"

"Oh, child, no," Miss Alaina chimed in. "Grandmother and Grandfather had five more children – three boys and two girls." She laughed as though telling a private joke. "Let me tell you something else about folks back then. They were color struck. Sister told you that Sarah and William were mulattos, children of two different masters, but what she didn't tell you was that a lot of those bastard children…"

Alarmed, Miss Claudette cried out, "Sister!"

Unruffled by her sister's outburst, Miss Alaina continued. "A lot of those children grew up color struck. Because they were, usually, very fair-skinned with light eyes, they felt more privileged than the other slave children, and they usually were allowed certain privileges that the other slave children were not allowed. I said all of that to say, Grandmother and Grandfather were no different. They married, had a lot of little yellow children, and encouraged their children to marry such that they also would have little, yellow children."

"Really…that's interesting. I wasn't aware that there was that kind of thing going on post-slavery, even though I'm very aware that it goes on now."

"Honey, people tend to want to preserve their color. Then there are some dark ones who hate the color of their skin and marry light-skinned, to hopefully change the color of their progeny."

Zora, obviously, either bored with the direction of our conversation or with my presence, began to brood. "Look, give this child the information she came for and let her get on with her evening. I believe her primary interest for coming here was to discuss the Harlem Renaissance, which, in actuality, we know very little about. We were mere children at the time and…"

"Sister, don't do that. Why don't you go sit down somewhere? Everything is not about you. You know, as well as we do, that you can't get to the end of a matter without talking about the beginning and the middle…first. As a matter of fact, why don't you have a drink and sit down right here." Alaina pat the cushion next to her on the chaise lounge.

Miss Zora wasn't happy about what had just been said to her, but she fixed herself a drink and sat down. Other than sad and mean, I couldn't figure her out. It was apparent she wanted to be a part of our discussion, but she took every opportunity to make some kind of jab at anything that was being said. I'd have to watch her for awhile before I could figure out exactly what was going on with her.

Miss Alaina then looked over at Miss Claudette, who nodded and suggested she continue with the story.

THREE

Before Miss Alaina could continue, I excused myself to go to the bathroom. I was thoroughly enjoying the story about their grandparents, but I was really hoping we'd get to the Harlem Renaissance part of their lives before I had to leave. It looked like there was no chance of that happening, though. I was going to have to make another trip back to visit the sisters.

As I made my way back to the parlor from the powder room, as Miss Claudette referred to it, I could hear Miss Alaina cussing up a storm. I didn't want to be rude and walk in during their, clearly, heated discussion, but I also didn't want them to think I was eavesdropping on them – even though I was. Miss Zora had made it very apparent that I was welcome in their home, but not for long. I didn't want to breach the little trust that the other two sisters had in me.

What wasn't readily apparent was whether or not Miss Zora was actually listening to Miss Alaina and

Miss Claudette, as they took turns talking to her.

"I don't know why you have such a problem with us telling Miss Shae Mother and Father's story. It's a beautiful story. They loved each other from the moment they met until they took their last breaths. Grandmother and Grandfather Butler's story is just as beautiful. Great-grandmother and Great-grandfather   Roberts' story is a lovely one as well. It's nobody's fault that you have a problem with them being told. Every time we try to talk about Mother and Father we have to go through this with you. Look, heifer, don't make me put my foot in your behind," Miss Alaina threatened.

"Look, sisters, we have a guest in our home and we need to act accordingly. Mother would not put up with us acting like this. And, you, Alaina, you better not lift your foot up to anybody in this house tonight. Well, if you could lift it, that is. You better not. And, Zora, you better not fight with Sister in front of our guest."

I could hear Miss Zora laugh, a laugh that came from deep in her belly. "Alaina, you better sit down somewhere. It would be a sight for that poor child to walk back in here and find you on your back because you tried to lift your foot up to me."

I guess the thought of it tickled all of them because I suddenly heard a chorus of laughter coming from the room.

I could also hear Miss Claudette whisper, "Zora, please, just this one time, let us tell our stories uninterrupted. We have nothing in our family to be ashamed of and if we do, we just won't talk about it, okay?"

I heard little more than an "umph" from Miss Zora. I thought this was as good a time as any to make my entrance.

As I rounded the corner into the parlor, Miss Alaina looked over at me as she took a sip from her cup. "Did you find everything okay?"

"Oh, yes, ma'am. It wasn't a problem at all. Your house is lovely."

"Thank you. I don't know why we didn't think to give you a tour before we made our way into the parlor."

Miss Zora looked at me disapprovingly. Miss Claudette noticed and drew her lips thin across her face as she discreetly shook her head from side to side at her sister. "Let's continue because we don't want to keep you all night with our stories. Now, where were we?"

"I think you were...I don't know. Miss Alaina had just told me about the birth of your mother, Lily Rose."

"Oh, yes, let's continue with Father's parents. Well, Grandfather and Grandmother Roberts were both born right before slavery officially ended in 1864 and both of their parents were slaves."

"I'm sorry, but excuse me. I thought slavery ended in 1863 when President Lincoln issued the Emancipation Proclamation?"

"Of course it did, but most slaves weren't aware that they were free or it wasn't 'really' official until the end of 1865, after it was ratified by the 13th Amendment to the Constitution." Miss Claudette paused.

"Okay, thank you."

"So, as I was saying, Grandfather's parents were Felix and Flossie. Now, of course, they took the surname of their master, which was Roberts. Both Great-grandfather Felix and Great-grandmother Flossie were born in Africa, in Guinea. They didn't come over on the ship together. Master Roberts brought her to his plantation after purchasing her for breeding."

"Like she was an animal…"

"Exactly, like she was an animal, but from that purchase came a union between her and Great-grandfather Felix. The story was told that he saw her as she was being unloaded off the back of a wagon. He fell in love with her that very moment. He made up his mind that he would be the one that would have her. That was something he knew he couldn't share with his master. Once Great-grandfather found out that Great-grandmother was also from Guinea, Africa, he wanted her even more because he felt that would help him to maintain his connection with the homeland, even though she was Fula and he was Mandinka, which meant they didn't speak the same tongue."

By now Miss Alaina and Miss Zora had downed two cups of herbal tea, laden with brandy, and were totally engrossed in the story, as was I.

"So, how did they communicate if they spoke different languages?" I inquired.

"Because they were from the same country, they knew enough of both languages to talk to each other, but only in private. On the plantation, in front of the master, you had to speak English. Great-grandmother Flossie was still young, about 15 or 16 years old and Great-grandfather was 19, so he worked at winning her trust by teaching her the little English he knew, by helping her out with her work in the field, and by giving some of his food and water to her during the noon break and again at suppertime. He had never been a problem on the plantation, so Master Roberts didn't pay that much attention to him; and the elder, female slaves were fond of him and knew he would be a good husband for Great-grandmother Flossie, so they talked him up to her. They told her she needed someone to protect her from the other male slaves. They reminded her almost every day that she and Great-grandfather Felix shared the same homeland. Much reminding was not required because Great-grandmother Flossie's heart ached for the Motherland and for her family that she had been stripped away from. She knew she would never see them again, so it was easy to see why she'd put all her hope and trust in Great-grandfather Felix."

I couldn't help myself. I had to interrupt again. "What were their African names?"

Miss Claudette took a sip of her second cup of herbal tea, laced with honey and brandy, and smiled. "Great-grandmother's name was Fanta, which meant beautiful day, and Great-grandfather's name was Jato, which meant lion. Of course, Felix and Flossie were the names given to them by Master Roberts, for no particular reason other than the fact that he had to name his property."

"That's so sad. They had such beautiful African

names. Great-grandfather Felix really was a lion – the way he was trying to get your Great-grandmother Flossie."

All of the sisters found that funny and chuckled a bit, even Miss Zora.

Miss Alaina, interjected, "What man isn't a lion? We were told Great-grandfather was a tall, muscular man with beautiful, silky black skin and white teeth. Great-Grandmother Flossie, we were told, was beautiful too. Her skin was as brown as cocoa and her teeth as strong and beautiful as ivory. Nothing has changed. Men still like younger, beautiful women. They did back then and they still do now."

"Oh, Sister, shush," Miss Claudette playfully hummed. "Great-grandfather and Great-grandmother were meant to be together. He really was just a child himself."

Anxious to hear more, I coaxed her to continue. "So when did they get married?"

"Oh, it wasn't quite that simple. Remember, Great-grandmother Flossie was brought there as a breeder. The elder women slaves had to come up with a way to convince Master Roberts to mate her with Great-grandfather Felix."

"What? Really? Like they were animals?"

"Oh, yes. Now, you know, those masters weren't really as smart as they thought they were. Every day, or so, one of the older women, who cooked for the family, would look out the window and make comments about how strong Great-grandfather Felix was, and then on another day she would talk about how hard of a worker Great-grandmother was. After a while Master Roberts evidently begin to think about the two of them together – Great-grandfather   Felix being a strong, young, buck and Great-grandmother being a young, hard worker. He probably reasoned he could get a number of children birthed by Great-grandmother Flossie because she was so young. Well, one night that old Master Roberts came down to Great-grandmother Flossie's shack with Great-grandfather   and told her she had to mate with him. Little did he know, that was exactly what Great-grandfather   was hoping for! Great-grandfather   didn't take her right then because he loved her, and he wanted to honor her. He told her to tell the elder women, so that they could prepare her for an African marriage."

"You're not about to cry are you?" Miss Zora leaned over and whispered to me.

"I think it's wonderful that he didn't just mount her like she was an animal. Master Roberts was so busy thinking about your grandparents as chattel that he couldn't see them as human beings capable of loving one another."

Miss Claudette continued. "You're absolutely correct, but that didn't stop them from loving each other."

"What was their wedding like? I mean, how did they even have one?"

"Honey, the next night, after Master Roberts had gone into his house for the night, all the slaves on the plantation went to the other side of the field, where they

21

couldn't be seen. They built a nice fire, cooked plenty of food, and danced and sang for hours into the night, and then they went back to their shacks. Except, this night Great-grandmother and Great-grandfather   went to the shack that they would now share. It had been fixed up and decorated by the elder women slaves."

"Was that a wedding according to the customs of either one of their tribes or something?"

"Oh, no, neither; the Mandinka marriages were basically arranged by family members, and then Kola nuts, a bitter nut, were sent by the boy's family to the male elders of the bride-to-be, and if they accepted, the courtship would begin from there. And as far as the Fula people were concerned, neither the bride nor the groom had to be present at the wedding ceremony. There might have been something called a koowgal, a cattle ceremony, where the bride's father gave one of his cows to the groom, and that legalized the marriage."

"Sister, don't be modest. Tell Miss Shae about the Fula girls."

Before Miss Claudette could say anything, Miss Alaina continued. "Those Fulani girls weren't necessarily expected to be virgins when they got married, even though they married really young. They were actually expected to come to the table ready, willing, and able and with lots of experience for their husbands. Honey, that's what I'm talking about! Those Fulani women were ahead of their time. Shoot, I know I'm Fulani because I always gave it up on the first date, if I liked my date right off the bat. What's the point in waiting?" Miss Alaina almost fell off her chair laughing.

Miss Zora had already made it abundantly clear that she was not a fan of love stories.

Displeased with what her sister had said, she abruptly jumped to her feet. "This is exactly what I was talking about earlier. Why does this young lady have to know that about you? You don't even care that she could leave here with the impression that we're all just a bunch of old sluts! Mother tried her entire life to make sure you had at least a modicum of class, that you were a lady, and she taught us that a lady is discreet. She doesn't put all of her business in the streets. I don't think I'll ever understand you."

Before Miss Alaina or Miss Claudette had an opportunity to calm their older sister down, she stormed out of the room, slightly staggering from her cup of "tea" that she had been sipping on.

Fireball that she is, Miss Alaina laughed at her sister. "Nobody's thinking about Zora. She's so uptight. I'm not going to apologize because I've enjoyed my life. As quiet as it's kept, I continue to enjoy my life, if you know what I mean. Why keep secrets? Life is too short for secrets. Don't you agree, young lady?"

Before I could gather my thoughts and respond, she continued.

"What could a person possibly do in their lifetime that has never been done by anyone else? Nothing! God has blessed us with life. I say, just live. I'll tell you what the problem is. It's just been too long for her. She needs to just get herself some…"

"Sister, okay, that's enough." Interceding on Miss Zora's behalf, Ms. Claudette put an end to her sister's tirade. "Miss Shae, I'm afraid we've taken up quite a bit of your time, yet we didn't get to what you came here for."

"Please, I've enjoyed every minute of your stories. When would I ever have the opportunity to get firsthand accounts of history like this again? You haven't wasted my time at all."

Now that I was more relaxed, I could see that Miss Claudette and Miss Alaina appreciated my presence in their home. As a matter of fact, I knew Miss Alaina thoroughly enjoyed the audience. I couldn't wait to get back to my apartment to tell my roommate about them.

"Sister, Sheriff Granger's shift ended long ago. I think we should insist that Miss Shae spend the night, after she has supper with us, of course. That's the least we could do. She shouldn't have to drive back to Birmingham tonight."

"Alaina, that's the best idea you've had today. Miss Shae, we'd be honored if you would grace us with your presence at supper, and then stay over until, at least, breakfast. Please accept our invitation."

"I couldn't...I don't want to put you through any trouble..."

Waving her hand at me, Miss Alaina quashed any idea I might have had about driving back to Birmingham tonight. "It'll be like a slumber party! We haven't had one of those in years. Right, Sister?"

"What about Miss Zora?" I knew she would

disapprove of me staying.

"Don't worry about her. She's stuffy at first, but she'll come around. She always does. And anyway, can't you tell by that smell that she's okay?" Miss Claudette inhaled as she stood.

We all began to sniff the air. From the aroma that permeated the room, we could tell supper was almost ready. By the time I made my way to the dining room from the bathroom, the food was being placed down the center of the table. Again, the table was formally set: water glasses, red wine glasses, white wine glasses to the upper right of the plate; a bread and butter plate with a butter knife; a salad fork and a dinner fork; a dinner knife, a salad knife, a teaspoon, and a cocktail fork, as well as a dessert spoon and a dessert fork. The only other time I'd ever seen a formal table setting was once when I went out to dinner with my parents. They would be very pleased to know that I was being entertained by hostesses that considered formal table settings an everyday way of life.

I almost bumped into Miss Zora as I turned to go into the kitchen to ask if I could help. She continued passed me to the table.

"Have you washed up for dinner?"

"Yes, ma'am, I have. Is there anything I can help with?"

"Oh, no, you're a guest in our home." She paused long enough to look me up and down. "I understand you're going to spend the night with us tonight."

"Yes, ma'am, your sisters insisted."

"Of course they did. Please, have a seat. Dinner is going to be served in just a few minutes."

"Are you sure I can't help with…"

I thought I saw a smile as Miss Zora turned to go back into the kitchen.

"I'm actually finished. Please, have a seat. Everything's on the table."

FOUR

I imagine life as a Roberts sister is still quite interesting, even at their current ages. Just a simple conversation appears to be a production. The sisters had spent the afternoon in the parlor drinking tea chased with brandy, as if that was part of their daily routine. They're all accomplished women, in their own right. They're all well traveled. They've all written books. They're all intelligent and extremely articulate. They're all cultured. Yet, with all of those accomplishments, and more that I'm sure I'm not aware of, it seemed like they had even more that they could do, even though they were older women now.

Dinner was great. In spite of the fact that they had sipped on brandy and tea all afternoon, they still had wine with dinner. I guess it's official, they are not teetotalers. Surprisingly, there was a great deal of laughter during our meal. The way Miss Zora stormed out of the room earlier in the evening I never would have imagined that she could be as lighthearted as she was during dinner. She talked, laughed, told jokes, made fun of her sisters and made me feel, almost, more welcome than either one of her sisters. To my surprise and pleasure, she continued the story of her grandparents.

"So, Great-grandmother Flossie and Great-grandfather Felix could finally love each other openly after Master Roberts, so garishly, put them together to mate. Master Roberts' plan worked well. Grandmother had three girls and three boys; he allowed them to keep the youngest girl, Tycee, and the youngest boy, our grandfather, Mason. Father said it broke Great-grandmother's heart to have her children taken away and sold. She never saw them again. He said it changed her. It wasn't just that her children were taken away; as an African woman, she knew that it brought a sort of glory, if you will, to her husband, to bare children for him – especially sons. To then have them taken away, she felt, dishonored him, especially because he was Mandinka. Great-grandfather was the progeny of the Mali Empire, which was known for the wealth of its rulers and the profound influence it had on West Africa. Great-grandmother knew that, so even more she wanted to bare him many children, many sons. Great-grandfather understood that they were not in Africa, that things were different, so he made every attempt to explain to her that it wasn't her fault and that he loved her no matter what.

She continued to work hard on the plantation, but she remained somewhat distant from Grandfather and his sister, who was about a year and a half younger than him. She was afraid to love them openly, because she felt at any moment they could be taken away from her. So, Great-grandfather made sure he gave them extra love."

I could barely contain myself. To have the privilege of hearing personal stories about slavery almost took my breath away. "That's so sad; the idea that she was afraid to love her own children. What about Great-grandfather Felix, did she distance herself from him, too?"

I saw Miss Claudette use her cloth napkin to dab at her eyes, while Miss Alaina sat with her eyes closed, shaking her head from side to side. They had to have heard this story many times, but it was apparent that it still distressed them.

Miss Zora went on. "They never stopped loving each other. Fortunately, it wasn't long before slavery ended. Grandfather was born in 1864 and Aunt Tycee was born early 1863; slavery ended in 1865, but it ended in Georgia in 1864 after General Sherman marched through the state. Great-grandfather convinced Great-grandmother that they should leave the Roberts' plantation, along with many of the other slaves that were leaving, and go further north, towards true freedom. Now, mind you, that plantation was all they'd ever known, in this country. It provided a sense of stability and protection, of sort, but at a serious cost, of course."

"Well, where did they go? But more importantly, how did they get there? Slavery may have ended, but from everything I've ever read, most Southern white people weren't happy about them being emancipated."

"According to Father, they traveled to Ohio by way of Tennessee and Kentucky, stopping at safe houses along the way. It was a long trip, and by the time they reached Ohio it was cold. Fortunately, there were abolitionists along the way that directed Great-grandfather and Great-grandmother to a safe house in Ohio until they could get on their feet. Grandfather told us that he stayed there until he was about 18 years old and then, against his parents' wishes, he moved to New York.

Growing up, we heard a lot about Great-grandfather and Great-grandmother from Father, because we had the pleasure of visiting with them several times as children.

"How did Great-grandmother Flossie deal with him? I mean, I know losing her children changed how she treated the two children she was able to keep."

"Oh, by then, it appeared Great-grandmother had seemingly recovered from losing her children, but Father said she always had a great sadness about her – even when she smiled."

"That's too bad. I would imagine that it's difficult to get over the loss of one child, let alone the loss of several."

"Absolutely, but Father had fond memories of growing up. He always said Great-grandmother Flossie was lovely. He recalled how she cooked meals for him and his brothers and sisters; how he ate out of her garden; and how she mothered him and his siblings. I think having grandchildren did wonders for her."

Miss Zora stopped long enough to leave the room and

return from the kitchen with a cake. Not just any cake, but a seven layer jelly cake. I had never seen anything like it before. I knew she was baking something because you could smell it throughout the house.

Miss Alaina stood up to clear the table, because, evidently, dessert could not be served with dinner dishes on the table. I stood to offer my assistance, but I was reminded that I was a guest and I was to remain seated, so that I could be served appropriately.

We hadn't gotten to the Harlem Renaissance yet, but we were getting closer. I was captivated by the wealth of history that the sisters possessed. Just imagine, they weren't that far removed from slavery, just enough that they could talk with their grandparents that were actually born before slavery ended. I wanted to come up with a way to use the precious information that was being shared with me, but how?

Miss Alaina walked back into the dining room with four cups and a coffee pot on a tray. "This may be hard for you to believe, but we're going to have coffee with our cake. And before you ask, no I'm not going to put liquor in mine."

I laughed, as did Miss Claudette and Miss Zora. Miss Zora sliced the cake and put a very generous slice on a saucer and handed it to me.

"Thank you. I don't think I've ever had this kind of cake before."

Miss Zora continued to slice the cake and place wedges on the china saucers in front of her sisters. "Grandmother…"

"Which grandmother," I blurted out.

"Oh, yes, uhm, Grandmother Roberts, her parents were Great-grandfather George and Great-grandmother Becka – free slaves."

Miss Claudette, who was eating her second forkful of cake, looked across the table at Miss Alaina. "Sister, was there ever such a thing as a free slave?" They both chuckled, as if a private joke had been shared between the two of them.

Miss Zora didn't scan the room with her icy glare. Instead, she joked and lightheartedly reprimanded both of them. "Of course there is. I'm going to free both of you to slave in the kitchen after dinner, so there. I don't want either one of you to interrupt me any further because I didn't interrupt either of you earlier." She paused, but only long enough to look across the table at her sisters. "I'm going to continue, if that's okay?"

Without allowing time for either Miss Claudette or Miss Alaina to actually reply, she continued. "Great-grandfather George and Great-grandmother Becka had been slaves on a plantation in North Georgia, but shortly before slavery ended their master gave them their freedom. Both of them were still relatively young, 25 and 26 years old. They only had three children at the time, none of whom were sold off, so they stayed on the plantation and worked for the master for about three years. They were actually able to save what they thought was enough money to travel. So they left the plantation for New York. They were determined their children would have an education."

"Could either of them read or write?"

"Not much, just enough to get by, which was more than most slaves. Their master had allowed them to learn because their responsibilities on the plantation included certain business transactions. We're not quite sure, exactly, what kind of transactions, but we came to our own conclusions and assumed it had something to do with weighing cotton or selling crops, and maybe even buying other slaves."

Miss Zora began to eat the generous serving of cake she had placed on her saucer. It was obvious that she savored it for more than just its flavor.

Careful not to speak as she ate, Miss Zora dabbed at the corners of her mouth after putting her fork down. "Miss Shae, every parent wants their children to do better than them. Great-grandfather George and Great-grandmother Becka were no different. They knew there were some Southern white folks that treated Negroes well, they worked for one. They apparently reasoned that there had to be some Northern white folks that would treat Negroes even better. The Union soldiers had shown themselves kind to the slaves. Plus, the North offered opportunities to their children that they knew weren't available to them in Georgia. They moved to New York and had three more children. So, they had a southern set and a northern set. The youngest child was a girl, Emma Clements, our grandmother.

She was the one that taught us that the principal part of the day was dinner. When she was growing up, Great-grandfather insisted that all of the children were present for dinner, as long as they all lived in the same house together. Great-grandmother took great joy in cooking for them too, and at least once a month she would make, as a special treat, a seven layer cake iced with apple jelly. The recipe for this cake we're eating has been in our family since our Great-grandmother. We only prepare it for special occasions."

I couldn't imagine why they would consider my being there anything special. When the truth was, their welcoming me into their home was what was special, but I was flattered nonetheless.

"Thank you. I also consider it a special treat because not only is the cake delicious, it has history. I really like that." I smiled as I finished my cake.

As they cleared the table, the sisters continued to treat me as a guest. After dinner we sat on their back porch overlooking their beautifully manicured backyard. We continued to talk for the next couple of hours, about nothing in particular. I got the impression that they were staying up far past their normal bedtimes to entertain me. So, after a little while, I announced that I was getting sleepy. Miss Zora and Miss Claudette said good night and headed for their rooms, as Miss Alaina escorted me upstairs to a beautiful, lavender room midway down the hall. She reached into the antique dresser drawer and handed me a beautiful pink, silk nightgown.

"Miss Shae, you can use this bathroom here in the room to wash your feet, if you don't feel like taking a shower tonight. There're also some extra toothbrushes in the medicine cabinet. Please, help yourself." With her head cocked to one side, she stood in the doorway of the bathroom and watched me. "Shouldn't you call someone to let them know where you are?"

"Oh, yeah, you're right. I guess I should call my roommate. Thank you for reminding me."

"Well, you know where the phone is downstairs in the front hallway. Feel free to use it." As she was leaving the room, she turned around in the doorway. "Miss Shae, I must say, my sisters and I have had a very enjoyable day. Thank you. Have a good night."

I smiled. "So have I, thank you. Good night."

FIVE

The next morning I was awakened by an amazing smell coming from the kitchen. As I sat on the side of the bed, the morning sun shined very brightly through the window. It looked like Sunday. It even felt like Sunday. I had to get up and get dressed, so I could get on the road back to Birmingham. Well, first I had to get back to my car, which I had forgotten was parked at the sheriff's office in downtown Jemison. It didn't surprise me at all to find that my clothes had been washed, ironed, and folded. There was no way for me to know which one of them did it or even when they did it. I never heard a thing.

As quickly as I could, I washed up and brushed my teeth with one of the packaged toothbrushes that I found in the bathroom. The food downstairs seemed to be calling me. You would think, after lunch, dinner, and dessert the day before, I might not want to eat another bite. I couldn't imagine what Miss Zora might be cooking that smelled so good. As I looked through my shoulder bag for a brush or comb, or even a rubber band, to do something with my hair, I thought about everything I'd been told the day before. It was almost like living a piece of history. I never had the pleasure of meeting my own great-grandparents. It was unfortunate, but it was what it was. I was one of three children, whose parents were both only children, whose parents had them late in life. That pretty much summed up my family history.

When I walked into the kitchen, I found Miss Zora standing in front of the stove.

"Good morning, Miss Zora. I hope I didn't keep y'all waiting."

"Good morning. I hope you slept well. The east side of the house can be a little drafty."

"Oh, no, I slept like a rock. I think I'm in love with that bed. It's the best sleeping bed I've ever slept on."

"I'll tell you the secret, if you promise not to tell Claudette."

It was nice to see a softer side of Miss Zora.

"Of course, I promise." Raising my right hand and putting my left hand on my chest, I played along.

"It's the down mattress pad…on top of a down-pillow-top mattress. Claudette thinks she's come up with something new, but the truth is that bed would be just as soft with just one or the other."

"I didn't even know you could get a down-pillow-top mattress or down mattress pad. I think I might have to invest in one of those pads for my bed. Oh, yeah, and who should I thank for washing and drying my clothes?"

"That would be Claudette."

"Where's Miss Claudette, anyway?"

"She's in the garden getting fresh vegetables for dinner. If you don't mind, would you let her and Alaina know breakfast is ready?"

"Where's Miss Alaina?"

"She's on the back porch reading the paper and having a cup of coffee." She smiled. "Just coffee…"

Opening the screen door leading to the back porch, I looked back at her and smiled. "Oh, okay."

As I stepped out the door, I could see Miss Alaina sitting on a large, cushioned rattan chair in the far corner of the porch reading the Sunday paper and drinking her cup of coffee. Actually, she looked more like she was studying the paper.

"Good morning, Miss Alaina."

"Well, hey there. How are you this morning?"

"I'm great. How are you this morning?"

Shifting her body in her chair, she looked at me. "Do you have to ask? I'm fabulous – every morning, just fabulous."

I laughed. "Of course you are. Miss Zora asked me to come and get you and Miss Claudette. Breakfast is ready."

"Oh, well, we better hurry then. Sister doesn't like for us to tarry when she's cooking. It can quickly become a very ugly scene. Let's go get Claudette." She put the newspaper and her coffee cup on the table next to her chair and jumped up as if she was a spry younger woman in her 30s.

We quickly walked down the stairs and then across the backyard. I could see Miss Claudette bent over in her gated garden, picking who knows what, in a large bibbed, straw hat.

Miss Alaina laughed as we approached. "Look at Sister. You'd think she was a farmer instead of an educated, well-traveled woman. I just don't get her sometimes. We could pay someone to farm for us, but Sister insists on doing it herself. It's beyond me. She almost looks like one of the slaves from our discussion last night. Look at her. Look at that sh…"

I put my hand over my mouth as I laughed. "Miss Alaina!"

"What?"

As she spoke, Miss Claudette looked up and waved at us.

"Good morning, Miss Shae. How are you?"

"I'm fine. Ms. Zora sent me to tell you breakfast is ready."

"Sister, please hurry. I don't want Zora to get upset this early on a Sunday."

Miss Claudette rolled her eyes as she picked her basket up off the ground and walked toward the gate.

"Please, Ms. Claudette, let me get that. Thank you for washing and ironing my clothes." I opened the gate and took the basket from her hand.

"Oh, that was nothing. You're welcome."

"Sister, let's get back to the house before Zora hollers at us in front of our houseguest. I don't want to have to deal with her today, especially before we go to church."

I was baffled. Miss Zora was in such a good mood this morning. I couldn't imagine her getting upset over nothing.

"But Miss Zora laughed with me this morning."

"So what, she's crazy." Miss Alaina looked over her left shoulder as she pranced ahead of us.

"Sister, don't say that. Zora's just a little temperamental."

Miss Alaina stopped and waited for us to catch up with her. She stood in front of me with her hands on her hips. "Young lady, don't let anyone ever tell you that you're temperamental. That's just a fancy way to say you're crazy. Zora is crazy, watch and see!"

"Sister, when we get to the house, please don't provoke Zora."

Miss Alaina seemed to sing as she said, "Okay, Claudette."

As we climbed the porch steps, Miss Zora glared at us through the screen door. She wasn't upset, but noticeably agitated. I didn't think it had taken that long for me to go get her sisters, but clearly it took too long for her.

"Breakfast is getting cold and you both know we have to take Miss Shae to her car on our way to church.

Surely going to the garden and reading the newspaper were part of the sisters' Sunday routine. Maybe it was my presence that was throwing things off-kilter. I didn't know, but I was ready to eat and leave. Miss Zora stepped to the side as we entered the door, as if she was our mother…or our drill sergeant.

"Wash your hands and let's finish eating so we can get to church on time."

Miss Zora   had cooked French toast stuffed with cream cheese and strawberries, scrambled eggs, and turkey link sausage. There was coffee, mango juice, chocolate milk, and water for us to drink along with our meal. Again, the fact that I was eating yet another fattening meal flashed across my mind. I had to get back on task tomorrow, but, for today, I would be eating stuffed French toast for the first time in my life, and enjoying it.

SIX

The ride back to Birmingham was pretty uneventful. I had two hours to think about everything that I had heard the night before. Okay, so I won't have any notes for my class Monday afternoon. Actually, I have notes, but no notes that I can use for my project. Nothing in them remotely mentions the Harlem Renaissance, but I'm sure I'm going to get there with the sisters. I would, instead, just discuss the details of our meeting: how the town was so protective of the sisters; how the sheriff interrogated me like a wanted criminal; how I was taken to the sisters' home; how eccentric and bohemian they all are; how they always serve meals with a formal table setting; and the general differences in their personalities. The more I thought about it the more that sounded like a great idea. I would discuss the process of getting to the part about the Harlem Renaissance. I think I can slide by with that this week. I would mention that, even though we hadn't discussed the subject of my paper, I could see the subtle influences of the Harlem Renaissance in their personalities and their everyday lives. I think that would be acceptable to the professor. I'll definitely have to discuss the Harlem Renaissance when I go back to Jemison next Friday after my last class. The more I thought about it the more excited I got about my oral presentation and the prospect of going back to see the sisters.

As I drove, I also reflected on the ride with the sisters from their house to my car: Miss Alaina had suggested I come back the next Friday to spend the entire weekend with them, to complete my class project, she said. I think they really wanted me to come back because they enjoyed entertaining and talking about their family. Miss Zora, on the other hand, had reverted back to the mean woman she had been early the day before. When she did speak, if I believed what she said during the car ride, I would have thought that she didn't want me to come back, but, somehow, I knew that really wasn't the case. Miss Claudette merely smiled as she drove the car, which, by the way, was a very pretty, older model, teal Mercedes Benz. As a matter of fact, it was the only teal Mercedes Benz I had ever seen and it was immaculate, inside and out.

Most of the ride to town was uneventful – probably because it was Sunday, a day that the Roberts' sisters held sacred. I guess I shouldn't have been surprised to find downtown Jemison looking abandoned on a Sunday morning. There were a couple of people, one guy jogging and a lady walking her dog, but not much else was going on. My car was right where I had left it, in front of the sheriff's office. Sheriff Granger wasn't working, so there was no chance that Miss Claudette would see him while I was picking up my car. Then again, there appeared to be only one church in Jemison, so Miss Claudette would probably see him there.

When I arrived back at my apartment, I was ready to take a shower and sit back and actually write two sets of notes from my visit, one set for what was actually talked about and another set to read to the class. Before I could unlock the door to the apartment, my roommate, Melodi, met me, pulled me in by my hand, and quickly closed the door behind me.

"Have you talked with Shukree yet? Last night he called here, like, I don't know, 20 times. This morning he's only called about six times. He is so mad! The first few times he called it was early yesterday evening. He wanted to know if you had gotten back from Jemison yet. Then he called back and he wanted to know if you had called to say what time you were going to get back. Around 10 or 11 o'clock that brother called here mad as heck. He accused me of lying for you. He thought you were with some other dude. I think he was sitting outside in his car earlier this morning. Girl, what is really going on?"

"What do you mean what's going on? I told you where I was going and I called you last night and told you where I was."

"So, you really were with those women in Jemison all night?"

I brushed passed Melodi as I walked into my bedroom. "Oh, now you gonna trip? You know good and well I was where I said I was. Where else would I have been? If I had been with some dude I would have told you that and if I had been with some other dude I wouldn't have stayed out all night with him."

"You better call Shukree. As a matter of fact, you know what? You don't have to call him. He should be calling again in a few minutes. That Negro is bugging – for real!"

I closed my bedroom door and went into my bathroom and turned on the shower. I wasn't ready to deal with Shukree yet. I sat on the side of the tub as I took off my shoes. I just couldn't deal with him after having such a good night. I shouldn't have to explain myself. He's just my boyfriend, not my husband. I told him where I was going and what I was going to be doing. I can't help that I ended up spending the night. I can't believe he called the apartment all those times looking for me. Any other night I'd be wondering where he was, not necessarily tripping about it, but I would definitely be wondering.

The knock on the door made me jump.

"What?"

"Shukree is outside parking his car. What do you want me to tell him?"

It didn't matter what I actually wanted to do. I guess now would have to be as good a time as any to talk with him. "Nothing, here I come."

At least he didn't try to beat the door down. I guess he had already lost cool points by calling as many times as he had, and then by coming over and sitting in the parking lot this morning. I was surprised to see that he didn't look mad as much as he looked nervous. Melodi had just opened the door for him as I rounded the wall and stepped into the living room.

"Hey, Shae, can we talk?"

I looked at him, with his fine behind. I almost smiled, but I knew that would make him mad because he would probably think I was acting suspiciously.

"Yeah, but I was just getting ready to take a shower."

He walked up close behind me and whispered in my ear as we walked into my room. "What's up, Shae? You tryin' to play me?"

I turned to face him just as he slammed my bedroom door.

"Why are you trippin', Shukree? I told you where I was going. You had to know it was going to take all day. It takes two hours to get there and two hours to get back, and then I…"

"You spent the night, Shae. Who'd you spend the night with?"

I stood and looked at him in defiance. Only one thought was going through my head at that moment: *He is just your boyfriend, not your husband. You don't owe him an explanation about anything.*

I took a deep breath because I didn't want things to escalate, not that I was afraid that something was going to happen; I just wasn't up for an argument with him. I was never up for one, but it seemed like we did more of that than anything else.

"Look, let me take a shower and I'll tell you everything."

Of course, that calmed him down. Just the idea of me getting naked seemed to sooth the savage beast in him, at least for the moment.

"Why you gotta take a shower, Shae? Who you been with?"

I walked up closer to him and kissed him on his lips. "Shukree, you know me better than that. I haven't even been with you. Why would I do anything with anybody else?" I gently took hold of his face and kissed him again. "Sit out here and wait for me. I'll only be a minute. Talk to me through the door while I take a shower, and then when I get out I'll tell you about my visit to Jemison."

Putting his arm around my waist, he pulled me into his chest. "You sure you don't want me to take a shower with…"

I put my finger on his lips. "Shhh, let's not go there, okay? Just sit down and wait for me. I'll only be five minutes, promise."

Shukree walked across the room, turned on my TV, and sat down on the bed. I quickly took my shower while he looked for anything on TV that was equal to sports. After drying off, I slathered on a little lavender and blackberry lotion, and then sprayed on just a little of the matching body spray, before slipping on a pair of panties and a sundress. When I walked back into my room, Shukree had kicked off his shoes and was lying across my bed. I stood in the doorway of the bathroom for a few minutes and watched him. Here he was 6'6", 230lbs, curly, black hair, hazel eyes, one of the stars of Miles College's basketball team, with his pick of the litter on campus and he was tripping because I was gone for one night. I liked Shukree a lot, especially when he wasn't tripping or lying to me about where he was those times I couldn't find him. I really didn't know where our relationship was going, but I did know that being with him kept the other guys away from me. I also knew that he did whatever he wanted to do with whomever he wanted to do it with. What I couldn't believe was that he thinks I don't know that. Miles is a small college, not much happens without everybody knowing about it.

I guess I had stood there too long thinking because he turned and looked over at me. Patting the bed next to him, he called me over.

Sitting up and fluffing the pillows on my bed, Shukree put them behind his back and leaned against the headboard and pulled my back against his chest as I sat on the bed next to him.

"Sit right here, girl, and tell me what you did in Jemison."

SEVEN

Shukree was happy; my professor was happy; and Melodi was happy. Shukree felt a little more secure about my trip to Jemison. If you can call asking to go to Jemison with me secure. My professor was happy with my doctored, journal notes and Melodi was happy that Shukree wasn't tripping anymore. I made him apologize to her for all of the harassing phone calls. I knew he blew her date that night. Just as sure as I was away all night, I'm sure she had someone up in the apartment with her. So, all those phone calls probably really blocked her plans. I had to promise her that if I ever stayed away from home like that again I would call Shukree to let him know where I was and that I would give him a number where he could contact me, if necessary.

The week couldn't go by fast enough for me. I called the Roberts sisters Thursday after my last class. Miss Alaina answered the phone. She told me Miss Zora and Miss Claudette had gone to Montgomery to take care of some business, but she didn't go because she and Miss Zora had a big argument. So, she stayed home to paint and drink her wine. She also told me that she and her sisters had been talking about me all week and that they were looking forward to me coming back on Friday. I told her what time my last class ended and when I thought I would be leaving, that way they could plan accordingly and keep an eye out for me.

I hadn't told Shukree that I was going to spend the weekend in Jemison, but I didn't think it was necessary because he had an out of town game. The team was leaving on Friday and coming back on Sunday. As far as he knew, I'd be at my apartment all weekend, like a good little girl. If he called while I was away, I told Melodi she could tell him that I had gone to Jemison. He didn't have to know when I left or anything like that. All he needed to know was that I was in Jemison.

As usual, on Friday, Shukree told me I didn't have to come to the gym to see the bus off. I'm not stupid. I knew it was because some other girl would be there. It didn't matter, though. I was probably going to be on the road to Jemison long before his bus left the campus. Sometimes I wondered why we even bothered dating each other. I know what his other girls are for. I made it clear to him from the very beginning – no sex. I would be a virgin until I got married. At least, that was my plan. He tries, but I think it's just to see if I really mean what I'm saying. I get it, really I do. He's a guy, so there's no doubt that he wants to have sex with me. I don't think I have anything to seriously worry about with him. He doesn't put a lot of pressure on me, so it works for me. I think that's why he really likes me. When we first started dating he told me that he respected me for not being like some of the other girls. I took that to mean they were "easy" and he kind of liked that I wasn't. I like him well enough, but I don't see us dating beyond college. If he makes the NBA draft, like he thinks he's going to, that's certainly not the lifestyle that I would choose to live; and, anyway, there will be a new line of women knocking at his door because he probably will have had all of the ones that he wanted from Miles College.

The ride to Jemison was beautiful. The sky was clear and blue. The clouds were big, white, and fluffy like cotton balls. I rode with my windows down and my radio playing loud. Going to see the Roberts sisters was like anticipating what was going to come next in a really good book. Miss Zora made me a little nervous because she's only mean or super nice, nothing in between; Miss Claudette and Miss Alaina are like, maybe, great aunts or even really cool grandmothers that I never had. I want to be friends with all of them, including Miss Zora, long after my assignment is over. I laughed out loud when I thought about what Miss Zora might cook for dinner. I made sure that I worked out every day to prepare for the eating frenzy I was going to have this weekend, starting tonight.

When I drove up, Miss Alaina was sitting on the front porch. She barely gave me time to get out of the car before she got started.

"I was about to get a little worried if you didn't arrive soon. Sister has been on the warpath all day. So there, you have been forewarned. And don't ask me why she's upset. It could be because the sun set a little earlier than she was anticipating or because the grass is a little high. We just give her a little space. Somehow, she usually finds her way into the kitchen. She works it out in those pots and pan. I don't know, but her being like this on a Friday is a good indication that the tone has been set for the entire weekend...or not. I don't know. Just stay out of her way and you'll be fine."

"Where's Miss Claudette?"

"She's in the house."

"Is she okay?"

"Sister is fine. Let's go in and let her know you've arrived. She'll be glad to see you."

Before locking my car door with the keyless entry, I grabbed my purse, my overnight bag, and my shoulder bag and walked up the porch steps to where Miss Alaina was holding the screen door open for me.

Pointing up the stairs, Miss Alaina instructed me, "You can put your things in the room that you slept in last weekend. Wash your hands while you're up there and meet us in the dining room, or experience the wrath of the Zora." She winked her eye before turning and walking away.

The dinner itself was lovely, just like before. I had never had squash prepared the way Miss Zora had cooked it. Nor had I ever had asparagus in a cream sauce or roasted chicken breast stuffed with broccoli, feta cheese, and roasted sundried tomatoes. Unlike before, dinner was uneventful, it seemed, because Miss Zora was not in a good mood. Miss Claudette and Miss Alaina were very tentative and precise in their conversation – not a lot of laughing, and no fanciful talk. I sensed that they were anxious, but I didn't know why. Several times during dinner I glanced up to find Miss Zora looking at me. I should have been the one that was anxious, but I wasn't. Unlike before, this time I tried to remain very conscious of everything I said and did. I didn't want to annoy her any more than she was already annoyed, or any more than necessary. Maybe her bad mood was because I was there again, but from what I could tell, though, all of them had had a good time the weekend before. That's why I was invited back.

Lifting a forkful of food to her mouth, Miss Zora spoke before taking a bite. "So, Miss Shae, tell me, how was your week? It's been a long time, but, if I recall correctly, college is very exciting and busy?"

"Yes, ma'am, it still is. The most exciting part of my week was doing my oral presentation for my project. The professor, as well as the class, seemed to enjoy it.

Professor Snead said he was looking forward to seeing how I develop my paper."

"Remind me, again, please, exactly what is the project?"

"Basically, I have to write about someone from the Harlem Renaissance and show how he or she was influenced by the era."

"Where do we fit in? I'm sure you're aware that we were just children during that time."

I looked at Miss Claudette and Miss Alaina to see if either one of them was going to come to my defense, but it was apparent that Miss Claudette was taken aback by her sister's attempt to humiliate me for no apparent reason, and, more than likely, Miss Alaina was either waiting for more ammunition before she intervened or she was hoping I could handle myself.

"Well, I think I mentioned last weekend that I ran across Miss Claudette's book in the library at school, so my plan was to do my project on her and explain in my paper why she was worthy of studying because of the subject of her book, which also included references to the Harlem Renaissance, which indicated to me that she had been influenced by the era, even if only a little bit. You and Miss Alaina are actually an added bonus." I twisted my lips to the side, awaiting her response.

"Sister, please don't be rude. It's apparent that you're very close to making our guest feel uncomfortable. Mother would be appalled at your behavior," Miss Claudette snapped.

For a moment, Miss Zora shrunk back. "Well, I just

want to make sure…"

Stomping her foot, Miss Claudette continued. "Sister! This young lady is not here to hurt us, and I refuse to believe that you are really convinced otherwise. Much like you did last weekend, make her feel welcome in our home because she is. We have had the benefit of living wonderful, exciting lives and we continue to be blessed with extraordinary experiences. We've shared so much with so many others throughout the years, I'm sure we have a little left to share with young Miss Shae.

Miss Zora stretched her neck and pursed her lips, as if to reclaim her dignity. She then exhaled and stood. "If we're finished eating, I'd like to clear the table and serve dessert." She then left the table with plate in hand.

After clearing the dining room table, it was decided dessert would be served in the parlor. Upon entering the room, it wasn't difficult to notice the stacks and stacks of photo albums and boxes, which, I assumed, also contained photos. I excused myself and quickly went upstairs to get my tape recorder.

Miss Claudette and Miss Alaina now came back to life – back to the sisters that I had the pleasure of meeting just a week before.

"Sister and I were busy all week looking through these photos. Oh, it brought back such memories. We laughed, we cried, we reminisced." Putting her hand over her heart, Miss Alaina closed her eyes and shook her head dotingly.

"It had been such a long time since we looked through our photo albums. Doing so made us remember things that we had no idea we'd even forgotten. We could hardly wait to share them with you this weekend. I have no doubt this will help your project or at least give you more substance regarding our background.

As they began to go through the pictures, Miss Zora walked into the parlor with a tray. There were slices of her rainbow sherbet pie, made with three layers of different flavored sherbets, whipping cream, pecans, and a crust of macaroons – another dish that I had never had before. For as mean as Miss Zora seemed to be, she sure could cook and bake her butt off. I thanked her as she silently handed me my piece of pie. Her eyes were almost apologetic.

Miss Alaina accepted her saucer from her sister and quickly directed her attention to the photos. "Sister, start with the photos of Grandmother and Grandfather Butler."

Miss Claudette grabbed a large, brown, suede photo album with gold embellishment, as Miss Alaina put a morsel of the pie in her mouth. "Sister, this is one of my favorite desserts. It's such a refreshing treat. Thank you for indulging us today." There was a twinkle in Miss Alaina's eyes as she smiled at Miss Zora.

"What would you ladies like to drink?"

Without hesitation, Miss Alaina responded first, "Sister, I would like a glass of Harvest White Riesling, please."

Miss Claudette was already leafing through the photo

album in her lap, so she didn't acknowledge her sister.

"And you, Miss Shae, what would you like, a cup of coffee?"

Before I could respond, Miss Alaina answered for me. "No, bring her a glass of wine too."

"Oh, Miss Alaina, I'm not old enough to drink..."

"What does that have to do with anything? So what you're not old enough. I'm certain you don't say that when you're drinking with your friends. And, anyway, you're here with us. Who's going to know? Surely you're not trying to impress us. Please, enjoy yourself."

"Don't let Sister corrupt you. She will, you know," Miss Zora smirked, as she turned and walked away.

EIGHT

Handing me each picture, Miss Claudette described, in detail, the scene in every one of them. "So, this picture here is after Grandmother and Grandfather Butler married. Mother told us that they were dressed because they were attending a Negro party, which was only attended by other mulattos."

"They were a good looking couple. Other mulattos, what was that about?"

Miss Alaina began her narration of things as she knew them, but only after first taking a sip of wine from her glass. "Child, I told you, Negros were terrible back then, after slavery. This color consciousness isn't anything new. It began with the slave masters separating the slaves according to the shade of their skin. The sad part was that all of them were just the same – just slaves. I'm sure they, the light-skinned ones, began to think they were better. It's hard not to think that if you're being treated better. Everybody, back then and now, wants to be treated well." She chuckled to herself, as if recalling some situation in her past.

After what appeared to be a pause for emphasis, she continued. "Light eyes, long hair, light skin all seemed to stand for something, for some reason – even if they were all just Negros who started in the exact same situation."

"But Miss Alaina, you're pretty fair-skinned yourself. Wouldn't you say that gave you certain advantages throughout your life?"

"I might be fair-skinned, but I'm the darkest of my siblings. And, you better believe, when I was growing up that was always brought to my attention by everyone I came in contact with. One of my father's friends used to call me "Little Blackbird." He even made a song out of it and sang it to me."

"You're not that dark, though, and you have long hair…"

The sound of Miss Zora's voice indicated she had finished cleaning the kitchen, with the exception of our saucers and glasses in the parlor. "Sister, don't have that child thinking you were forsaken as a child. You were just as privileged as Claudette and I. And you used your long hair and big eyes to your advantage, as often as you could. I'm almost embarrassed to say that you still shamelessly use your looks to your advantage." Ending her comment with a laugh, Miss Zora sat down with a glass of wine in hand.

Consequently, Miss Claudette joined the conversation again because it had gone astray. "At this rate, we're never going to finish looking at all of these photographs. It's a good thing you're spending the weekend, Miss Shae."

With that said, we looked at pictures of the Butler and Roberts families until 1:30 in the morning. We were able to go through hundreds of pictures of their grandparents on both sides of their family, as well as photos of their uncles, aunts, and some of their cousins. Yet, we never quite made it to the Harlem Renaissance that night.

I need seven hours of sleep, no more, no less. I didn't get in the bed until about 2:00 a.m. and now, right at the crack of dawn I could hear a lawn mower. What is the world coming to when you can't even sleep late on a Saturday morning? I couldn't imagine which sister would be up so early in the morning cutting grass. If I had to guess, though, I'd say it was Miss Claudette. I got up and drug myself over to the window.

At first glance, it was obvious that it wasn't one of the sisters. As a matter of fact, it wasn't even a woman. Whoever it was, he was tall, dark, and fine. Partially shielded by the curtain, I stood in the window and watched him as he rode the mower back and forth across the yard. The muscles in his arm flexed as he turned the steering wheel and his wife-beater t-shirt clung to his sweaty chest and back. It was apparent that he worked out. He had another white t-shirt tied around his head. I wanted him to stop the mower and stand up so I could see how he was wearing those jeans he had on.

"What are you peeking at, Miss Shae?"

Startled, I jumped as I turned to find Miss Alaina standing in the doorway. "I'm not...I heard...I was just looking out the window."

"Uh, huh. He fine, ain't he?" She laughingly teased as she walked away. "Get yourself together. Breakfast will be ready in about 20 minutes, and you know how Sister is."

It didn't take me long to get dressed. I showered as quickly as possible and discreetly rushed downstairs to find out who that was outside cutting the grass. Miss Zora was in the kitchen. Politely as I could, I hurriedly greeted Miss Zora and went out the kitchen door to the back porch to find Miss Alaina.

"Good morning, Miss Alaina."

"Well, good morning, again. How are you this 'fine' morning?" She smiled as she turned away and looked at the guy out in the yard.

"I'm good. Who is that cutting the grass?"

"That's Shiloh," She almost sounded like she was singing his name.

"Shiloh? Really?"

"Really. You should get to know him. You and he would make a really cute couple."

"Miss Alaina, I have a boyfriend."

"Uh, huh, yeah, okay. What does that have to do with what you do here? And anyway, do you really only have one boyfriend?"

"Of course, how many am I supposed to have?"

"Well, when I was in college, I had a boyfriend back home, one on campus, and an older boyfriend off campus."

I didn't even know how to respond to her dating revelation. Miss Alaina sounded like she used to either be very progressive or an h-o-e. "Why would you need so many boyfriends? I mean, really, it sounds so complicated."

In her slow, precise drawl, she began to school me on the skills required to date several men at one time. "Oh, please. It wasn't that complicated at all. I went to college at Howard University in Washington, D.C., and my boyfriend back at home wasn't going to come there to visit because I went home to visit him every few months. My campus boyfriend and I were both poor college students, so we spent most of our time together on campus. We might have gone to a movie in town every now and then. Now, my boyfriend off campus was a little older than me, so he took me on sophisticated dates. You know, out to dinner, to museums, to shows, and he kept a little money in my pocket."

"Miss Alaina, you were fast." Grinning from ear to ear, I half-heartedly joked with her.

"Hell, yeah I was fast. I wasn't going to be left behind. There was too much to see and do in Washington, D.C. I liked all of my boyfriends, though. I didn't see why I had to only have one. Honey, it took three men to handle me anyway." She laughed reminiscently as she sipped from her cup of coffee, and then lifted a joint up to her lips.

Miss Zora hollered from the kitchen. "Sister, watch your mouth and don't you corrupt that child with your stories or your marijuana."

"Sister, you know as well as I do, college is about experimentation. It's where you find yourself through new experiences. And Miss Shae is no longer a guest. She is company," she hollered back.

"So, Miss Alaina, how'd you do that and how long did you date all three of them?"

"What you're really asking me is was I having sex with all of them; right?"

I thought I was being discreet. Her insight caused me to blush. "Yeah, I guess so."

"Look, this is how I see college then and now: You go off to college to get a degree; you get there and you know how to wash your clothes. You actually already know how to learn because that's what got you into college in the first place. So, college is really about two things: learning who you are and exercising your sexual freedom. Ultimately, college is really for – sexual freedom."

I looked over at the door and Miss Zora was standing there leering disapprovingly. "Sister, you're going to have this child thinking we were all a bunch of loose women when we were younger."

It amazed me that Miss Alaina was so candid about sleeping around when she was younger, but I guess there was nothing to hide at her age. It had happened and it obviously wasn't something she regretted.

"Sister, if you're still concerned about that after all these years, let me clear it up for you now. Miss Shae, my sisters were not only good girls when they were in college, they were also monogamous. I was the only one that didn't have any sexual hang-ups and I still don't. In some circles I may have been referred to as a slut, but those are the people that can kiss my...."

"Sister!" Miss Zora thunderously stomped her foot as she censured her sister.

Miss Zora's outburst neither startled Miss Alaina nor swayed her conversation, as she continued. "So look here, your boyfriend back at school is probably a nice boy. Are y'all having sex?"

I wasn't expecting that question, but I shook my head from side to side.

"Well, let me assure you, he's probably having sex, lots of sex, with other girls when you're not around, so you better try to get with Shiloh. He's just like you. He's really nice too." With a nod of her head, she then took a long pull from her joint.

Miss Zora shook her head as she turned and walked away from the screen door. "Breakfast is ready. Miss Shae, you and Sister can come in and eat."

Miss Alaina snuffed out her joint in the ashtray on the table next to her chair, and then stood up and looked out toward the yard. Just as she was about to call out to Shiloh, Miss Zora appeared back at the screen door.

"Sister, I said breakfast is ready. I'll take something out to Shiloh. You know I'm not going to let him in my dining room after he's worked out in the yard. Don't test me this morning."

The sisters locked eyes after Miss Zora said what she had to say, and then turned and walked away from the door…a second time.

NINE

After breakfast we sat in the living room to go through more photos. Finally, today would have to be the day that we talked about the Harlem Renaissance. I was sure of it. Miss Claudette, Miss Alaina, and I found our respective spaces and got comfortable. Miss Zora walked into the room as she slipped her right arm into the sleeve of a very nice, pastel colored sweater.

"I have an errand to run. I'll return shortly. Does anyone need anything from town?"

"What errand, Sister?" Alaina asked, as she walked in her sister's direction.

Miss Zora smiled. "I won't be long. I should be back by lunch time."

It was apparent that Miss Zora wasn't going to tell anybody where she was going and it was even more apparent that Miss Claudette wasn't going to exert any further effort to get her to divulge what her errand might be.

"With all of these great pictures, why don't y'all have any pictures of your family hanging on the walls around the house?"

The sisters looked at each other. "Even after all of these years, it's still difficult for Sister," Miss Claudette uttered, almost unintelligibly.

I looked at Miss Alaina. She responded, as if reading my mind. "Not me. Zora."

"What is it that's still difficult for her?"

My curiosity was piqued by their air of mystery because nothing had previously kept them from speaking freely. Miss Zora had left the house, so there was no chance of her walking in on us. Miss Alaina excused herself, but quickly returned to the room with a beautifully decorated, green, velvet covered photo album. It was then that I recalled that I was there for more than just a weekend getaway. I excused myself and ran upstairs to get my tape recorder. When I came back, I turned it on and sat it on a table that had the least amount of photo albums on it.

Opening the velvet, photo album, she pointed to a picture of a really good looking white man holding an adorable light-skinned, little black boy.

"Who is that?"

With pained expressions, Miss Claudette and Miss Alaina looked at each other. Eventually, Miss Alaina responded. "It's Hervey and belle fils – Zora's husband and son."

"Her husband and son; I'm confused? Where are

they?"

Miss Claudette wiped at her nose with a napkin. "Hervey and our nephew, belle fils, beautiful son, as Sister used to call him, were killed in a terrible car accident many, many years ago. I don't think Sister ever really recovered."

That explained a whole lot. "So, she never wanted to remarry?"

Miss Alaina sucked air through her clinched teeth. "Who ever really knows anything when it comes to Sister? What we do know, though, is that she loved Hervey. She lost her virginity to him when she lived in Paris and shortly afterwards she married him. Sister dated all through Wilberforce, but refused to have sex with anyone. She introduced us to Hervey when we went to visit her in France. That was how we found out she was married."

"Lived in Paris? What was Miss Zora doing in Paris?"

Miss Claudette laughed. "Haven't you wondered why she cooks all of the time? After she graduated from Wilberforce, she went to culinary arts school, Le Cordon Blue, in Paris, and then after graduating with a Grand Diploma she cooked in one of the finest restaurants there. And that is where she met Hervey – Hervey Poulet.

In the restaurant, she was a novelty, of sorts. The only Negro, female sous-chef in Paris at the time, and the youngest, I believe. It was a beautiful story, actually. Hervey was a patron at the restaurant one night. He so enjoyed his meal that he asked to meet the chef – Sister. He told us, when she came to the table he could not believe that the hands that had prepared his delightful meal belonged to such a beautiful woman. He came back several nights in a row after that. One night, he finally worked up the nerve to ask her out. Shortly after their first date, Sister fell in love. She wrote and told us about him. Her exacts were, *I found my husband*. Now, what she didn't tell us was that Hervey came from a very affluent family. They owned several wineries in the Normandy countryside. After they were married, Hervey put Sister up in a beautiful countryside chateau and about a year after that she gave birth to Gustave, belle fils."

It would make perfectly good sense that, at least, one of the sisters married a white man, particularly since they're part white. But I would never have guessed Miss Zora, maybe Miss Claudette. Definitely not Miss Alaina.

"It sounds like Miss Zora had a very exciting life. I mean, living in France, graduating from a famous culinary school in Paris. That explains a lot."

Laughing aloud, Miss Alaina hooted, "Like, why Sister can cook her behind off!" She continued to laugh as she spoke. "She can cook or bake anything you can dream up. Honey, take my word for it. She can do it."

"Oh, I believe it. And what is a, uhm, 'sue chef'?"

"A 'sous-chef' is the chef that's second in command in the kitchen."

"And what is a Grand Diploma?"

Miss Claudette chuckled to herself as she continued,

"That diploma is the core of the Le Cordon Bleu's curriculum, and the most rigorous and comprehensive education program in classic French cuisine and pastry techniques available today.

I believe those were the happiest days of Sister's life – when she was working at that restaurant and when she was married to Hervey. Of course, when we came back to the States and told Mother and Father that she was married, Father was not pleased at all. He wanted to know what kind of man would marry a woman without meeting her parents first. His mind changed after he met Hervey – even though Mother and Father didn't meet him until after Gustave was born. Mother thought Sister's courtship and marriage to Hervey was quite romantic. She never fretted over it one bit. When she saw how happy Sister was she was happy too. She knew her oldest daughter wasn't impetuous – like her youngest. But, unfortunately, because of the racial climate here in the States, it was much safer for Sister and Hervey to remain in France. It was his home anyway and Sister was very happy there."

For a moment she paused, it appeared, to gather her thoughts. "Alaina, please, let's put Sister's photo album back where it was before she returns. It would be an absolutely horrid scene for Miss Shae if she walked in on us."

"Who is this pretty lady?" I asked, pointing at a black and white photo.

Very proudly, as if singing a verse from their favorite song, the sisters responded simultaneously, "*Mother.*"

"Oh, my goodness, I see where all of you get your good looks from. She was drop dead gorgeous!"

Pointing at the picture of a tall, statuesque, black man, who I knew had to be their father, Miss Alaina introduced him. "And this is Joseph Earl Roberts, 'my' father." Her voice went up an octave, making her sound almost childlike. She must have been his favorite.

Showing me another picture of them together, Miss Claudette spoke fondly of her parents. "Father absolutely adored Mother. She could do no wrong in his eyes, but Grandfather Butler never liked Father –"

"He was too black! Grandfather never liked him – never!" Miss Alaina exclaimed.

Miss Claudette's eyes smiled, "No, Grandfather never appreciated that Father had the audacity to even approach Mother. After all, she could pass for white. But, oh, my goodness, Mother and Father loved each other madly and had a good time with each other. They loved each other hard – as hard as Grandfather hated Father. It never mattered to the two of them, though. And when Father sat down at his piano and played it *Harlem Style* and mother opened her mouth to sing. Oh, my word, it was absolutely extraordinary."

Laughingly I asked, "So I take it they partied during the Harlem Renaissance?"

"Honey, that's not even the word for it. Our house was alive with music and merriment from sunset on Fridays until the sun rose on Sunday mornings. The house was littered with musicians and singers in one room, writers and poets in another, and painters and artists of all sorts mingling in between. People danced all over the place. Mother started cooking as soon as she got home from her teaching job. She told us how, early on, Father had convinced her to cook and sell plates for $1.00 and a cold drink for another .10¢. If you wanted liquor, the rule was you had to bring the bottle yourself and you had to be willing to share it. Father was very innovative." The beautiful sound of laugher bellowed from Miss Claudette as if she was clinging to fanciful memories. For a minute I thought she was going to jump out of her chair and start dancing.

Equally as excited, Miss Alaina chimed in. "It was a titillating time! Father always danced with me first, and then one dance each with Zora and Claudette before we were sent to our rooms. Afterwards, Mother would sneak biscuits with jelly back to us. I don't think she was really sneaking them, but the idea that she might have been simply added to the allure of the night for us."

"So, how did your house become the party place? No, let me backtrack a little bit. How did your mother and father meet?"

The sisters looked at each other and smiled. This was, no doubt, another one of their, often repeated, favorite stories. If it was even possible, they perked up a little more.

Miss Alaina could barely contain herself. "Sister, you tell her – tell her."

Miss Claudette began the story. "Well, all of our

grandparents had migrated to the North because they heard that the opportunities for Negros were much better there – Chicago, New York, you know. Grandfather and Grandmother Roberts traveled to Chicago and Grandfather and Grandmother Butler to Albany, New York. Now, the Roberts were hardworking folks from Georgia, so Grandfather Roberts chose that area because of the work he had been told he'd find there – work that would allow him to take care of his family the way that a man should take care of his family. Grandfather Butler, on the other hand, though he was a hard worker, and wanted to have a house full of children with Grandmother, he wanted to go where he had heard Negros could make it big. He was a dreamer, you see. The sky was the limit according to him. He and Grandmother Butler had no problems finding work."

"They had that damn light skin," Miss Alaina chimed in.

"Watch your mouth, Sister."

"Well, they did."

"Unfortunately, Sister is right, but Grandmother was also smart. She taught Grandfather to read and write while they were courting and she continued teaching him for a while after they were married. So, because of that, the fact that they were two very fair-skinned Negros that could read, they didn't expect to have any problems at all. Grandmother Butler found a job in an exclusive dress shop; Grandfather Butler, well, he found himself a job waiting tables at an equally nice restaurant. Grandfather worked hard, bought a car, and then one day surprised Grandmother with a little house. Not long after that Mother was conceived. When she was born she was so beautiful to Grandfather that all he could think of was his favorite flowers back in Alabama – lilies and roses, so mother was named Lily Rose. A year later another daughter was born, Aunt Amaryllis Marie. They tried for a boy, but got Aunt Jasmine Lorraine. So Grandmother tried once again to give Grandfather a boy, but then came Aunt Chloe Louise.

Now, while this was going on in Albany, Grandfather and Grandmother Roberts were in Chicago working just as hard, if not harder. Grandfather worked in a factory and Grandmother worked as a housekeeper. They lived in one of those shotgun houses."

"I'm sorry, Miss Claudette; remind me, what is a shotgun house?"

It would only make sense that Miss Alaina would respond because they did a great job of taking turns when they spoke. "It's a narrow house that you can stand at the front door of and shoot a shotgun out the back door. But first, let me tell you something that Father was proud of. He said Grandfather Roberts built a hallway from the front room to the back room, so that you didn't have to go through all of the rooms to get to the back of the house."

"Why would he have to do that?"

Miss Alaina responded. "Because the damn rooms were back to back – the living room, then a door to the first bedroom, then the second room, the third room, and then the kitchen. So, Father said Grandfather built a hallway down the left side of the house, built walls and a doorway for each room, except the living room and the kitchen. They ended up having three completely private bedrooms and one bathroom. As they grew up, Aunt Angelina had her own room and the boys shared a room. As a little boy, Father said he was proud that they were, probably, the only shotgun house in the neighborhood that had a hallway.

Grandfather worked for years at the factory until he became a foreman, over the Negros, of course. And Grandmother quit her job after she had her first baby. She then stayed home to raise the children, grow fresh vegetables to feed her growing boys, sew Aunt Angelina's clothes, and wash and iron other people's clothes to bring a little extra money into the house. Father said Grandmother Roberts used to say, 'As long as your papa is pulling then I'm pushing.' So, they lived a good humble life."

We had gotten so engrossed in the storytelling that we didn't realized that we'd been sitting there for over two hours. So, it was as good a time as any to take a break. "Miss Claudette, Miss Alaina, I don't know about either of you, but I'm a little thirsty."

Miss Alaina stood up and walked passed me, headed for the kitchen. "Well, I tell you one thing, young lady, if you want to spend another night here you better not go in that kitchen messing with things, unless you know exactly what you're looking for. We told you Sister used to be a chef. She doesn't take lightly anybody fooling around in 'her' kitchen. Let me go in there with you and show you how to do this. Anything we touch we have to wash, and we have to put the kitchen back just like we found it."

"Oh, okay."

I couldn't remember how long it had been since I last heard the humming of the lawnmower. I walked over to the back door and looked through the screen. I wondered where "what's his name" was. No sooner had the thought crossed my mind when he came from around the house towards the stairs.

"Miss Alaina, here comes that guy."

Without stopping what she was doing, she quickly glanced over her shoulder, "Who, Shiloh? Is he still out there? Good."

"What's good about that?"

"I can introduce the two of you."

"Miss Alaina, I told you – "

"Told me what? What?" she quipped, playfully.

Shiloh appeared at the door before I could remind Miss Alaina that I had a boyfriend. He greeted me and then acknowledged Miss Alaina.

"Miss Alaina, can I come in for a second and get something to drink?"

"Sure, Shiloh, I want to introduce you to our friend anyway."

I stepped to one side as Shiloh excused himself and walked through the doorway passed me.

Miss Alaina quickly stopped what she was doing, grabbed a towel, and wiped at her hands. "Shiloh, this is our friend, Shae Leslie. Miss Shae, this is Shiloh

Manuell Shaw, III, our neighbor," and then she turned
back to what she was doing.

"It's nice to meet you. I would shake your hand, but
as you can see I'm dirty and sweaty." He smiled as he
looked down at himself.

"It's nice to meet you too." I maintained eye contact
with him as I spoke. Even though, I was really fighting
the urge to stare at how his sweat, soaked t-shirt clung to
the muscles in his chest. There was no doubt, Mr. Shaw
was finer than fine – all of that grass cutting had done
him well, and his blinding white teeth were
unbelievable.

"Miss Shae, would you please get Shiloh something
cold to drink? The glasses are here in the cabinet in front
of me, to my right." Miss Alaina's voice seemed to come
from the other room, even though she was standing right
there in front of me.

"Miss Shae, the glasses are right here," Miss Alaina
repeated as she motioned to the right with her head.

I didn't realize I was daydreaming. "Oh, okay. Yeah,
I can do that."

Every glass in the cabinet was as pretty as the next. I
didn't want to give him one of Miss Zora's best, but it
looked like they were all her best. I grabbed a brown
tinted glass with a black handle – it looked more like a
fancy misshapen, beer mug. It seemed to be the
appropriate glass for a hardworking, young, black man.
It fit him, brown, strong, and nice to look at.

Opening the refrigerator, I gazed inside to see what
there was to offer. "What would you like to drink?

There's mango juice, orange juice, milk—"

"Water is fine."

I stood in the opened door of the refrigerator as I poured him a glass of water out of a clear glass carafe. He had stepped so close to me that I almost hit him in the chest with the glass as I turned to hand it to him.

He looked down at me and smiled. "Thanks."

Over his left shoulder I could see that Miss Alaina had turned her attention away from the kitchen counter and was looking at me with a mischievous smirk. Shiloh turned the glass up to his mouth and held his head back to drink, I watched his throat as his Adam's apple moved up and down with each swallow he took – I think I swallowed too. I then found myself looking at his chiseled chest again, as well as the muscles in his arms and shoulders. He smelled sweaty, but he didn't stink. I inhaled and, for some reason, found myself swallowing along with him again.

Looking pleased by what she saw, Miss Alaina smiled and turned back to what she was doing at the counter. "Shiloh, why don't you come back and join us for dinner tonight. Claudette and Zora would love having you – that is, if you don't have other plans. I'm sure Miss Shae would appreciate having someone closer to her age present, as well." She paused briefly. "You know what? Even if you do have plans, change them and, please, come back and join us. You know me. I'm not going to take no for an answer."

Shiloh laughed as he stepped back to let me close the refrigerator. I laughed, nervously too.

"Miss Alaina, it would be my pleasure. What time is dinner?"

Without turning to look at him, she sang, "Sister usually starts dinner around 5:30 or so. Please arrive around 5 o'clock. If dinner isn't ready by the time you get here, we can sit on the porch and talk until it is."

He responded as he walked towards the door. "Okay. That sounds good, Miss Alaina. Let me go back outside and clean up, so I can get on with the rest of my day." As he touched the screen door handle, he turned around wearing a broad smile across his face. "Miss Shae, it was nice meeting you. Oh, and thanks again for the water."

"You're welcome. Shae – call me Shae."

"Thanks, Shae. See you later on this evening."

When the door slammed behind him I spun around to find Miss Alaina standing behind me holding a tray of drinks and snacks.

"What?" I asked her.

"Nothing…" She then turned to go back into the other room where Miss Claudette was waiting patiently for us.

"He's fine, aint' he?" Her words left a trail in the air.

Without answering, I quietly followed behind her.

TEN

Miss Zora didn't say much when she returned, besides, "I'm getting ready to prepare lunch. You all need to have this mess cleaned up by the time I finish."

Rather than continue, Miss Claudette thought it best that we put the pictures away for a while and perhaps get back to them after dinner. Concerned, she whispered to Miss Alaina that she thought Miss Zora was unusually upset. I couldn't tell the difference. It looked the same as all of the other times I had seen her upset. Fortunately, the only thing we had to do was put photos back in their respective boxes and then stack the photo albums and boxes in a corner of the parlor. We had stopped earlier to clean the dishes from our snack.

After cleaning up, I went upstairs to look for an outfit for dinner, only because the sisters insisted I dress for dinner this time. It shouldn't have mattered because my boyfriend is playing a basketball game – and I didn't have to be cute for anyone else, in spite of what Miss

Alaina had said earlier. Shiloh is really fine, though. If he looked good dirty and sweaty, I could only imagine what he might look like all cleaned up.

I laid my clothes out on the bed: a long, snug, denim skirt and a real cool psychedelic halter, and then I went back downstairs to see if I could trick Miss Zora into talking to me while she prepared lunch. I was intrigued by her life story, the fact that she had been married and had a child, and that she had actually lived in France, as if visiting France wasn't exciting enough. I knew I was going to have to be discreet, because she would be really upset with Miss Claudette and Miss Alaina if she knew they had told me her business.

As I stood in the doorway between the dining room and the kitchen, I silently watched Miss Zora. I couldn't put my finger on it, but something didn't seem quite right. She stood in front of the open refrigerator far too long. If she had been stooped down looking for something or if she was even doing more than just standing there, I wouldn't have thought twice about it, but she was just standing there. Finally, movement, she closed the refrigerator door and walked over to the kitchen sink. She braced herself on the counter and looked out the window over the sink. Afterwards, she walked back over to the refrigerator, opened the door, and grabbed a jar. It was then that I thought I should make my presence known.

"Bonjour, Madame Zora. Qu'est-ce que tu cuisines?

Puis-je vous aidere?

"Oh, no, I have it, but thank…you…"

For a few moments she stood very still. I could hear her breathing as she looked down at her hands.

"Who told you…how did you know…? How can I help you, Miss Shae?"

I didn't know if she was angry or just caught off-guard. It wasn't my intention to offend her. I just wanted her to talk to me like her sisters do, especially now that I knew a little more about her.

"I thought you might…I thought I might be able to help you with lunch."

"Miss Shae, I'm not sure what went on here today while I was away and I'm not going to ask, but don't think that you're here to do any more than complete a class paper. I'm certain that my sisters have made it clear to you that the kitchen is my space, my private space, and that I won't tolerate any type of intrusions."

As Miss Zora stood facing me with her arms across her breast, she closed her eyes and took a deep breath, as if exasperated. "Mademoiselle Shae, obtenir la vaisselle de l'armoire, s'il vous plait. Le rose et le blanc Wedgewood Bone China. Merci."

Smiling, I walked over to the cabinet to her left. "Certainement. Mon pleasure."

Lunch was surprisingly pleasant. Miss Zora kept glancing at me, but she never mentioned anything about our earlier conversation in the kitchen. I almost expected her to reprimand her sisters for telling me she spoke French, but it never happened. We all laughed and talked about the pictures of their mother and father, and about how much fun the sisters had as children.

Caught up in the revelry, Miss Alaina jumped from her seat at the table and began to dance to music only she could hear. "Zora, do you remember how they danced all night…"

Laughing, Miss Zora joined in. "…telling stories and reciting their poetry. It was certainly the best time. Sisters, do you remember Gwendolyn Bennett and her short story, *Wedding Day?*"

I sat back and listened as she began to recite it, verbatim:

"His name was Paul Watson and he shambled down rue Pigalle. He might have been any other Negro of enormous height and size. But as I have said, his name was Paul Watson. Passing him on the street, you might not have known or cared who he was, but any one of the residents about the great Montmartre district of Paris could have told you who he was as well as many interesting bits of his personal history. He had come to Paris in the days before colored Jazz bands were the style. Back home he had been a prize fighter."

"To this very day, I still love that story. Hmph…"

She seemed to suddenly lose herself in reverie of a very happy time for her. I was even caught up in how electrified the room had become.

"Miss Zora, I mean, really, what was it like...for you?"

Smiling, she began, "Now, keep in mind, we were just children, but we could tell it was something special – the Negro Diaspora. In the words of the great Duke Ellington, 'It was like the Arabian Nights.' To be Negro during that time was in vogue. There was fanfare and merriment – always! I heard one of the writers; no, I think it was mother that I heard, on one occasion, refer to it as delicious. It was a delicious time. Artist wandering from place to place – clubs, flats, apartments. Music playing, intellectuals amongst the writers, amongst the singers, amongst the poets, amongst the just regular Negros; you know? It was a really good time for the Negro in Harlem. And they weren't just your run of the mill Negros, even though there were a lot of them there too. Negros came from Chicago, Washington D.C., Ohio – all over – just to be a part of what was going on in Harlem. It was just the kind of atmosphere Father loved, and that Mother grew to love."

I was about to burst at the seams because it sounded like one big party. "So, was it like that all of the time or just on the weekends?"

Gleefully, Miss Claudette now added her harmony to the story. "Oh, as we later learned, the clubs were like that every night. People came from all over New York to listen to Duke Ellington, Bessie Smith, Count Basie, Thelonious Monk, and I'm sure some others you probably aren't so familiar with, Fess Williams, Noble Sissle, Nora Douglas Holt Ray. They kept the –"

"Cotton Club?"

"Oh, no, Miss Shae. Movies would have you believe we were at The Cotton Club, but the Cotton Club was for the whites that wanted to be entertained by our talented Negros. We actually spent most of our time on Jungle Alley, where there were several other nightclubs and cabarets. Negros also spent a lot of their time at the speakeasies."

This was a history lesson I couldn't have paid for. I was hearing about people and places I had never heard of in my life. "So, what happened at the speakeasies, lots of partying, huh?"

Tired out by her gyrating and shaking, Miss Alaina sat back down. "From what Mother told us, the speakeasies are what invented partying. The people could buy cocaine and marijuana there for almost nothing, and it seemed like quite a few indulged heavily. One of the most famous spots was the Sugar Cane, which was in a cellar. Father took Mother there a few times, but, of course, that wasn't Mother's kind of place, which is why they started having their own rent parties when they found out about them."

"Rent parties?"

"It's just what it sounds like. Rent was high in Harlem, so they had parties to pay the rent. Mother and Father usually had their parties on Saturday night – when Negros who did domestic work were off. Now, the night might have started off with music from the radio, but eventually someone who could play a musical instrument would show up – a saxophone, and then, maybe, a drum and a guitar. It was a given that someone there could sing. Like we told you earlier today, each room had something different going on: in one room they might be playing cards; in another they would be dancing; in another they might be in their drinking and 'philosophying'; and, of course, there was always one room that was just off limits to us children. At the time, we had no idea what could have been going on in there…"

"What was going on…"

Miss Zora laughed louder than I had ever heard her laugh on either one of my visits. "Miss Shae, do we really need to tell you?"

"Oh…ohhh, really? Your mother and father didn't mind that?"

"How were they going to control it? A lot of the people that came there were already drunk or high, not everybody, mind you, but quite a few were. With all of that dancing and rubbing up against one another, it was only a matter of time before human nature ran its course. And let me tell you, that chemistry between men and women is strong! And then you had the added nuance of liquor and drugs. Who was going to stop them?"

"So there was lots of sex?"

Miss Zora continued. "The word 'lots' is an understatement. During that time in Harlem it was very hedonistic. People came there to let their hair down, to unwind from their boring lives and to be whatever they chose to be in the dark night of the Harlem lights."

"So, how did your mother and father escape all of

that?"

With her chest poked out, Miss Alaina spoke, "I heard Father got caught with a woman or two…"

"…two," Miss Zora added.

Rolling her eyes at her sister, she continued. "Father was a fine looking black man. I could only imagine how difficult it was for Mother to keep him under control or to keep those women away from him. To be honest with you, I actually walked in on him one time. Mother had put us down for the night. She'd given each one of us our biscuit with jelly and a glass of milk. Sometime after she left, I had to go to the bathroom. Now that I think back, a considerable amount of time had passed and Zora and Claudette had fallen asleep. I wanted to wake Zora, but I was in a tight and I didn't have time to waste trying to stir her awake. So, I crept through the crowd. The air was thick and smoky and people were everywhere. They didn't pay the slightest bit of attention to me. I didn't see Mother or Father, but, then again, I wasn't looking for them either. All I knew was that I had to get to the bathroom, and then back to my room. As I approached the bathroom door I could see that it was slightly ajar. By now I'm about to use the bathroom on myself. So, if you could imagine, I'm holding myself between my legs with one hand and with the other I push the door open. Even the bathroom was filled with smoke, so I couldn't immediately make out who was in there, but I could certainly see that the man's back was to me, his belt was unbuckled, and his pants were down. I could also make out a lady sitting on the sink with her legs straddling him. Well, the lady saw me and whispered something in the man's ear. When the man turned around, I realized it was Father!

I didn't know what they were doing, but I knew he shouldn't have been hugging and kissing on any other woman besides Mother. He grabbed at his pants as he asked me what I was doing there and if I was all right. I was so shocked that I pissed right there on the floor, in my pajamas. And with that, I started crying. It took Mother about a second to make her way into that bathroom. Imagine, amidst all of that commotion, she could hear her baby crying. By the time she got in there, though, Father had fixed his clothes and that ugly lady was standing there next to him...looking at me, like she felt sorry for me! Mother picked me up, looked at Father and took me to my room and changed my pajamas before putting me back to bed."

Miss Claudette giggled, "That's how Sister became Father's favorite. They shared a very big secret that he was afraid she might share with Mother. Sister, did you ever tell Mother?"

Huffing, Miss Alaina scrunched up her face. "Of course not – I didn't know what was going on, but I could tell it hurt Mother terribly. The next day, I heard them in the kitchen whispering about it. Mother was giving it to Father for allowing me to see him in such a compromising position. Of course, Father apologized, but never admitted doing anything wrong."

"Mother loved Father something awful. She had to have known what he was doing, but I believe she told him it better not happen again. Father loved Mother so much…"

"He stopped fooling around?" I inquired.

"No, he kept it away from home. But as we grew up we knew. Well, I knew. I could tell by the way women hugged him or held his hand too long, or how they touched his arm. I loved Father, but he made it very difficult to trust him…"

"…for Mother, of course," Miss Zora scornfully interjected.

The conversation seemed to be taking a turn for the worse, so I knew I had to say something to ease the tension. "If you had to sum up the Harlem Renaissance in one statement, what would each one of you say?"

Miss Zora spoke first. She smiled as she stood to clear the table. "C'etait magnifique!"

"I'd have to say, even as a child I found it electrifying and deliciously decadent." Miss Alaina added, as she exited into the kitchen with dishes in hand.

Miss Claudette, on the other hand, sat back in her chair. "I'd have to say, it was a time that everything, literature, poetry, music – absolutely everything – was about plain Negros' day to day lives. Our struggles, as unappealing as they may have been, were brilliant and very poetic, not just to Negros, but to the whites as well. The Harlem Renaissance certainly wasn't for the timid at heart. It was a liberating and enthusiastically, energetic time that paved a way for our Diaspora from the indignity and dreadfulness of the rural south to the splendid wonders of the north."

"I know you all were just children, but, aside from the rent parties in your home, is there anything else you can tell me?"

"Well, let's see, one more thing." Miss Claudette's eyes searched the air as if looking in the corners of the room for more to say. "Oh, I think it was mentioned that it was supported by Negros. If I didn't, I certainly meant to. There were more than just clubs. There were Negro-owned businesses and publications, and just like the clubs, the businesses were also frequented by whites. Don't misunderstand me; Negro support was pivotal to keeping the mystique of the Harlem Renaissance alive. The most interesting aspect of the Harlem Renaissance, though, was the fact that, as much as whites enjoyed our culture, they still considered us "primitive.""

"What do you mean by that?"

"Exactly what it sounds like, they considered us less developed, which is why we have been so exploited. Our creativity was exploited then just as it is now. Our ingenuity was and continues to be exploited. Our intelligence was and is exploited. Do I have to mention our physical prowess? All exploited. Sometimes we act to our own detriment, though, because we want the notoriety, the celebrity, the money, but most of the time exploitation occurs because someone else sees the brilliance in our being. We used to see it. Not so much anymore, though.

I mean, just think, Miss Shae. You and I have ancestors that survived slavery. That was an absolutely, undeniably, phenomenal feat. They actually survived one of the most horrific times in American history and, in addition to that, we have ancestors that then managed to survive all the mistreatment that came after slavery. There is brilliance in our being." She smiled. "It took intelligence and ingenuity to survive the many atrocities that they suffered, such that you and I can actually sit here and have this conversation today. That same brilliance led us to the Harlem Renaissance, where our creativity was on the forefront.

Yet, on those occasions when we act in such a way that allows us to be exploited, it's only because we're demanding, requesting, and expecting equality. It's the same now. We are most mistreated when we speak up and request that we be treated equally and humanely. The Harlem Renaissance allowed us recognition in the mainstream of society. It allowed us to 'almost' feel a sense of humanity because there is humanity and peace in creativity, in artistic pursuits."

I nodded because I not only understood but agreed with what she was saying.

Miss Alaina and Miss Claudette looked at each other and smiled, as if they shared a special secret, and then Miss Zora reminded them, "And in spite of everything, it was a happy time, until the Stock Market crash, which occurred in 1929. After that it was pretty sad because everyone's money was gone, including the money that kept Harlem alive. It slowly became poverty stricken."

"I really should know this. "How long did that last?"

Miss Claudette looked at Miss Zora. "The Great Depression ended around 1935. Is that correct, Sister?"

Miss Zora merely nodded.

ELEVEN

Miss Zora shook her head from side to side as she wrung the cloth napkin she was holding. "I was a little girl, about six or seven years old, but I still remember Father and Mother doing a lot of whispering. I remember folks coming by talking to them about white folks committing suicide. Everybody was worried because the factories were shutting down, the clubs and restaurants were closing, and everything was going out of business. I didn't know what it was at the time, but people kept talking about something called 'Black Tuesday.' I had no idea what that could be.

Sisters, I don't know if you all can recall any of this because you are so much younger than me, but do you recall Mother crying and asking Father what they were going to do because the bank didn't have their money anymore?"

Both Miss Alaina and Miss Claudette shook their heads from side to side.

Miss Zora continued, "I knew it was something terrible. I could just tell from the tone of the voices of all of the adults. Mother cried a lot and Father kept hugging her and reassuring her that we were going to be okay. She thought we should pack up everything and move South, but Father didn't want to do that."

She stopped speaking and stared off to her right, as if lost in her childhood memories, and then as quickly as she had stopped she began again.

"Father was a city boy. He liked the music of the night, those fast women, that fast life – he liked all of that. Now, mind you, Father didn't drink, smoke, or do drugs, as far as we know, but he loved being around those fast talking, lying types. Father's best friend, Henry Brown, was a gambler and a liar, and Father loved that man. How was he supposed to let go of all of that to go back to the South? Never mind you that, at one point Mother was the only one working. She was a teacher and little Negro children still needed to learn.

The restaurant where Father had waited tables fired all of the Negro waiters, busboys, and cooks, and hired unemployed whites. As a matter of fact, whites were hired and Negros fired from any job that whites had previously refused to work. For a while it was extremely difficult for us, for more than the apparent reasons. There were whites who felt like all Negros should go back down South and pick cotton."

Baffled, I interrupted her. "Excuse me, Miss Zora. I don't remember learning about this in any of my history classes – the part about black people losing their jobs like that during the Depression. I mean, I know people lost their jobs because businesses closed, but this is the first time that I have ever heard that black people were forced off of their jobs...because they were black."

Miss Alaina had apparently sat idly by for as long as she could. "Shoot, of course you didn't learn that in any of your classes. All of the books written for schools would have you believe that the only thing of any importance at that time was that people had lost their money, white people; that businesses had closed down, owned by white people; and that people were killing themselves, white people."

This time Miss Zora didn't even bother reprimanding Miss Alaina for interrupting her. Instead, she continued with her story. "Oh, that was nothing, honey. Negros were actually murdered for their jobs."

I glanced over at Miss Claudette, but she sat with her head tilted to one side, her hand over her mouth, her eyes closed.

So, I looked back at Miss Zora. "What? I mean, why?"

"I have asked myself that same question many times over the years, for many reasons, but I eventually came to learn that there's only one answer: because people can be evil and heartless. It was bad up North, but it was even worse down South. In Georgia and Mississippi there were campaigns against Negros with jobs. If I recall correctly, I think it was in Atlanta, there was a group similar to the Klan that called themselves the Black Shirts. They actually..." She stopped for a brief moment, as if it was too painful to continue. When she appeared to gather her composure she continued. "Well, they actually went around saying, 'No jobs for niggers until all white men had jobs.' And in Mississippi there was an incident where a mob of unemployed white men ambushed a train and killed all of the black men that were on the train working."

As I listened, I attempted to search my memory to count how many history classes I had taken over the years. I didn't know how this newfound information would impact my life or if it should have an impact on my life in any way, but it would have been nice to grow up more aware of my actual history as a young black woman in America. It made me sad to hear that, once again, we were the target of unwarranted attacks...just because of the color of our skin.

"Well, back to Father. Even though his job had been taken from him, eventually – because most people weren't working – nobody was going out to eat anymore anyway, so the restaurant closed down. Before the Great Depression, waiting tables had been good money. Not only was it good money, it was an honorable job. After Father lost his job, for a little while, he hung out a little bit too much with his friend Henry Brown. Mother didn't like that. To be honest with you, I didn't like it either because Henry Brown was a slick talker. He was nothing like Father. Though, before things went bad, every now and then Henry Brown would bring us candy and little sweet cakes. One time he even brought dolls for each one of us. That's how you knew he had gambled the night before, and won. I also think Henry Brown knew he wasn't that likable. Mother was worried that Father was going to go off with him and gamble away the little money she was able to stash away. Even though it never happened, she still worried about it. Father found little odd jobs from time to time and when he got paid he always managed to bring home a little treat for each one of us – a piece of rock candy, black licorice, or cookies, and he gave the rest of his money to Mother."

As all of the sisters sat silently, smiling to themselves, they appeared to ponder over a difficult, yet happy time in their lives. I hated to interrupt their reverie with my words, and I had no idea how long it would be before one of them would actually say something, but, as I sat there with them, it occurred to me that it was most probable that each one of them had her own way that she remembered the events in their shared childhoods. Yet, the results for all three of them ended up being the same. They had all grown up to become beautiful, happy, interesting, artistic, eccentric, intellectual, worldly women who adored their parents.

After lunch Miss Zora and Miss Claudette excused themselves and went to their rooms to take naps. Miss Alaina cornered me and asked me to go for a walk with her. I made sure that I had my tape recorder with me as we exited the kitchen door and walked across the backyard towards the tree line. When we reached the middle of the yard, Miss Alaina stopped walking and turned and looked at me.

Looking around playfully, she chuckled to herself. "Shiloh did a good job with the yard; don't you think? Uh, huh..."

I looked at her, not knowing what to expect next: like, perhaps, Shiloh jumping from behind a bush or something. Nothing happened, though, so I answered her question. "Yeah, I suppose so."

In her best sing-song voice she teased me. "Shae and Shiloh sitting in a tree – k-i-s-s-i-n-g!" As we continued walking towards the thicket, she laughed hard from her belly.

As soon as we entered the woods, Miss Alaina pulled a joint from her pocket.

"You can't be serious?"

She looked at me as if baffled by my question. "What?"

I tilted my head to one side and looked back at her and pointed to the joint in her right hand. "Uhh…"

"Child, please! I've been smoking weed since college. There's no sense in stopping now." She smiled as she lifted the joint to her lips and lit it.

I watched as she inhaled the smoke deeply into her lungs and held it, and then coughed after releasing it.

"Whoa, this is some good stuff. I've had it here at the house for a while, but this is the first little bit that I've gotten out of the bag."

She was talking to me like it was all right for her to smoke weed in front of me. I mean, it's not like she was one of my friends on campus…because, of course, that would be okay – they're just kids. I'm sure she and her sisters inhaled quite a bit of marijuana during those parties her parents had, but I just couldn't, for the life of me, imagine Miss Claudette or Miss Zora ever smoking.

"Miss Alaina, do your sisters know how much weed you smoke?"

She came to a sudden stop on the dirt path we had begun to walk down, exhaled, and then blew the smoke upward toward the sky.

"Of course they do. I don't keep any secrets from them. And anyway, what are they going to do about it? Uh, huh… I'm respectful. I don't smoke it in the house. I smoke on the back porch or out here in this place I'm about to share with you. Uh, huh…"

Taking the half of a joint that she was still holding between her pointer finger and thumb of her right hand, she pressed it up against a tree and put it out, and then put the roach in the pocket of her sundress.

TWELVE

We walked down the path until we reached a clearing. It was like walking from one scene into another. There was a small body of water, too small, I thought, to be a lake, but too big to be what I would consider a pond. Directly in front of us was a boardwalk that extended out into the water. I followed as Miss Alaina walked to the right, in the direction of a large, covered deck. It wasn't just a covered, wooden deck; a portion of it was screened in and, from what I could tell as we approached, it appeared to be no less decorated than the house. Strategically placed on each side of the stairs were flowering bushes and across the front of the deck were four large, shiny, green and brown flower pots with beautiful cascading plants dripping from each one of them. It was like a picture in a magazine.

Miss Alaina stopped and dramatically turned around to face me as she touched the ornate door handle. "Miss Shae, welcome to what we fondly refer to as 'le porche belle eau.'"

"Oh, the beautiful water porch?"

"Ahh, so you speak French. Yes. Of course, Sister named it. It's a nice quiet place for us to come to when we need to get away from each other. Sister says I mess up the sanctity of the porch and miss the spirit of what it was meant for when I come out here to smoke." She stopped for a moment and laughed out loud, at nothing in particular. "Forget about her! She still tries to treat me like a child. I'm a grown woman." She laughed out loud again. "I come out here and relax the way that I want to relax. Don't you think that's fair, Miss Shae?"

I smiled. "I would love to come out here to take naps. It's beautiful." For the moment I had managed to avoid answering her question.

She then waved her hand in the air. "Please, make yourself comfortable, have a seat."

I plunked down on the off-white, overstuffed cushions of a beautiful, rattan loveseat. "This is great. If I lived here I would be out here on the water every night. I'd probably sleep out here. What's the name of the lake?"

As Miss Alaina took the roach from her pocket, I watched as she searched for something to light it with. "Do you have some matches or a cigarette lighter?"

I was tickled that she would ask, so I gave her a really broad smile. "Of course I don't. I don't smoke."

"I know you don't, you're a good girl...just like my sisters were." She walked across the deck to a little stand with a lamp on it and pulled the drawer open.

"Found one."

Miss Alaina held up a thin, purple, cigarette lighter, as if she had found a prize. She then proceeded to light what was left of the joint that she had begun to smoke during our walk to the lake.

After taking a couple of tokes she coughed then smiled. "You sure you don't want to hit this, Miss Shae? I'm going to finish it off."

I shook my head no.

"So, you had asked me a question. What was it?"

"What's the name of…"

Miss Alaina continued. "…this lake? The name of this lake is Lake Limihkachi."

"You made that up." I laughed at what I thought was her attempt to amuse me.

"No, ma'am, I did not make that up. The Alabama Indians that lived in this area named it Lake Limihkachi. It means shimmering waves of light."

"That makes sense." I turned and looked out at the water. "It does shimmer." And it really did. It actually sparkled as the sun shined on it.

I turned back to face Miss Alaina, just as she was removing the remnant of her cannabis cigarette from her lips. I waited until she exhaled. Eyes closed, she titled her head back and blew a cloud of smoke into the air. Fortunately, a gentle breeze was blowing across the deck, so the smoke quickly dissipated, helping me to avoid a contact high.

"Miss Alaina, how do you know so much?"

For a few seconds, with her eyes still closed,

contemplating her response, she leaned forward and propped her elbow on her thigh, balled her hand in a fist and placed it underneath her chin.

Speaking slowly, she began. "Miss Shae, our parents were lovely people. They made learning really important to us because it was important to them. When we were little girls, they read to us and they took us places, but of course, only to places where Negroes were allowed to go. And you know what?"

I shook my head from side to side, but then realized her eyes were still closed. "Uh, uh...no, ma'am."

"Our parents encouraged us to not only be inquisitive but to nurture our individual characteristics. That helped us to become the women that we are – the artistic women that we are. It also helped that they exposed us to different artisans as we grew up. I mean, really, we were fortunate enough to meet people that are now considered some of the greatest Negro authors, poets, artists, and musicians of their time. And, you know, we were just little girls, so we had no idea how much those things would influence us or what it meant to be in their presence."

She hadn't completely answered my question, but I could listen to her talk on and on because the aristocratic way that she spoke was entrancing. It was clear that they didn't grow up rich, but you couldn't tell when you were listening to her.

"And after high school, each one of us was sent to college. Because I have always walked to the beat of a different drummer, I went to a different college than

Zora and Claudette. They went to Wilberforce in Ohio and I went to Howard in Washington, D.C." She sighed deeply. "Later in life, long after our parents had died, after our travels, after all of our wonderful life experiences, we decided to move to Alabama together. So, we came down to Jemison to look for a house. I researched everything I could about the area. We couldn't find a house that we liked, so we bought this parcel of land that included this beautiful lake. The locals told me stories about the land and the lake and the rest is history.

So, to answer your question, I don't know if I know a lot, as much as I know a little about a lot of different things. Now, if you ask me about men, I can tell you everything about them. Speaking of which, tell me about your little boyfriend back at Miles College. What's his name and what's his claim to fame?"

"His claim to fame; I don't understand."

"What attracted you to him?"

"Oh, okay. Well, his name is Shukree…"

"Shukree, what kind of name is that? Oh, please excuse me. I'm really not trying to be condescending because I've dated guys with unusual names too, but I've never heard the name Shukree before."

"No, I didn't take it like that. I'm not sure where his name comes from. I've asked him about it, but he doesn't seem to know either. Let's see, what else. Oh, he plays basketball…"

"Basketball star, I hope – or else there's no point in dating him, unless it's just for the sex. I dated a couple, well, a few basketball players when I was in college. The sex was great…with most of them. Who am I kidding? It was great with all of them. When I had boyfriends in college, if the sex was bad I broke up with them. What am I saying? I'll break up with a boyfriend now if the sex is bad!" She laughed extra hard.

I think it was the weed, so I sat silently gazing at her, but only because I had never met anyone so open about sex. Even my friend Melodi didn't talk about it like Miss Alaina did, and Melodi was as loose as they come. I guess I had never known anyone Miss Alaina's age that was so willing to talk about any and everything so freely.

"Miss Alaina, I'm a virgin, so it's not for the sex. But, yes, he's, like, the star of the team."

"That's good then, but I'm going to give you some advice, and this is only my opinion, of course. Unless you really think your boyfriend is going to be a professional basketball player, and if that means anything to you, then you're investing a lot of time and energy into someone that other young women are willing to do whatever it takes to be with. I know from whence I speak. I was one of those young women, except I didn't want the guy to leave his girlfriend. I just wanted to spend time with him, and then move on to the next one.

I don't know what your relationship with Shukree is like now, but unless you're willing to have your heart broken over and over again then you might want to think seriously about why you're dating him. All of my cynicism aside, I'm sure he's nice to you. He's probably really tall and handsome and you two probably make a beautiful couple, but I'm sure you could have anyone else that you wanted. And I'm sure I don't have to tell you that you wouldn't have to deal with as much aggravation as you deal with right now."

I tried not to show it, but I could feel my face drop a little. She was right. Every time I turned around there was some other girl trying to get with Shukree, and I can't even say I'm surprised by that. I know he's having sex with other girls. He only tries to have sex with me every now and then, and I know that's just to test me – to see if I mean what I say. I only date him because it keeps the other guys from bothering me. When they approach me, the few who don't already know, I tell them I'm Shukree Williams' girlfriend and they back off.

I gave her a half smile. "Yeah, you're right. I don't consider our relationship too serious. It's not like I want to marry him or anything like that."

"And it shouldn't be serious. You're in college! What did I tell you before? College is a time for you to express your sexual freedom…"

"Well, I don't know about all of that, but I do think it's a time when you become more independent and you learn more about yourself."

In the distance, I thought I could hear Miss Zora calling out, but it couldn't have been. It seemed like we had just started talking.

Apparently, Miss Alaina heard the same thing. "Miss

Shae, it's been a lovely visit, but I think dinner is ready."

THIRTEEN

Miss Zora didn't even turn around to look at us as we walked through the kitchen door. "Shiloh will be here shortly. Both of you need to clean up for dinner."

I glanced over at her, but I didn't respond. The smell coming from the kitchen was more than I could take. How could someone so mean make the house smell so good? As I followed Miss Alaina up the stairs, I had to ask, "What's Miss Zora cooking in there? I have never smelled anything like that before in my life."

Miss Alaina stopped, looked back over her left shoulder and waved her hand towards the kitchen. "Who knows, with you and Shiloh joining us for dinner tonight, I'm sure we're having a four course meal." She then turned and continued up the stairs, with me following close behind.

We had all showered and changed clothes by the time Shiloh arrived. I had never dressed for dinner before, even though all I was wearing was a denim skirt and a halter. I had never stopped what I was doing and actually showered and changed clothes just to eat. It was kind of neat, though.

We hadn't been sitting in the parlor long before there was a knock at the front door. I motioned to stand up to go answer it, but Miss Zora stopped me.

"Miss Shae, you're a guest in our home. You shouldn't answer the door. Let Sister do it." She looked over at Miss Alaina, who was sipping on a little, before dinner cocktail.

"What? Let Claudette do it."

Miss Zora looked at Miss Alaina disapprovingly. Without saying a word, Miss Alaina took another quick sip from her drink and stood up to go answer the door. When she stepped back into the parlor she was arm and arm with Shiloh. She was also carrying a bottle of wine.

She held the bottle of wine out in front of her, "Look at what Shiloh Manuell Shaw brought with him. He is such a gentleman."

Almost on cue, Shiloh Manuell Shaw greeted us.

I could not have imagined him looking any better than he did earlier in the day, but he did. All he had done was taken a shower, put on a crisp, white, button-up shirt, another pair of dark blue jeans, and splashed on a little cologne. He smelled better than he looked. His black skin against his white shirt almost took my breath away. I tried not to stare, but I'm sure I was.

"Hi, Shae."

"Hi, Shiloh." I tried not to smile too big.

Out the side of my eye, I could see Miss Alaina smiling.

From the kitchen Miss Zora called out, "Dinner's ready."

I didn't even realize she had left the room.

We all made our way into the dining room. Of course, Miss Alaina escorted Shiloh, arm and arm, as she ushered us to our assigned seats.

"You two young people sit across from each other. I'll sit right here next to you, Shiloh, and Claudette will sit next to you, Miss Shae."

The table setting was extraordinary. Miss Zora was using some plates that I had not seen before. As a matter of fact, I had never seen plates as pretty as the ones she had on the table. They were green with gold trim. A dark green, vine design with pink flowers decorated the middle of the plates, but the most striking design was the red bird in the center. The coffee cups and the saucers had the same pattern. Miss Zora had also put three wine glasses on the table for each one of us. One of them was filled with water. As we took our seats, Miss Zora walked in with a tray. Shiloh stood to help her.

"No, please, take a seat. I have everything under control. These are just appetizers."

As she placed the tray in the middle of the table, Miss Claudette asked what we were all curious to know. "That looks delicious, Sister. What is it?"

Miss Zora looked the happiest that I had seen her since we met. "This, my dears, is shrimp satay with mango ginger sauce. The shrimp were marinated and then grilled on coconut palm frond skewers, and are being served in a mango ginger sauce."

I could have eaten just that for dinner. I looked up from the tray to find Shiloh looking at me. I blushed and quickly looked at Miss Zora.

"Please, everyone, help yourself. What can I get you all to drink? We have Moscato, which is a sweet white wine, and Cabernet Savignon, a red wine."

I asked for the white wine because my past experience with red wine had not been a positive one. With the exception of Miss Alaina, everyone else asked for white wine too. Miss Zora removed the tray that she had served our appetizers on. She left the room then returned with two bottles of wine.

"So, Miss Shae, Shiloh, what do you think of the appetizer?"

It was obvious Miss Alaina was trying to get us to talk. Because the food was so delicious, we all had our faces in our little saucers, quietly stuffing them with shrimp.

"I don't' know about Shiloh, but I have never had shrimp like this before. I usually just have it fried."

Shiloh grinned, "Me either. Before this evening, I would have said fried and steamed was the only way that I ate it." He laughed out loud and we all joined in.

I looked in Shiloh's mouth. I don't know which was

whiter, his teeth or his shirt. The white t-shirt that peaked from underneath his shirt was white too. I silently compared him to Shukree. He was just as tall as him, but he smelled better. I didn't mean to, but I laughed out loud.

"What's so funny? We want to laugh too."

I hadn't notice before, but Shiloh's eyes were kind of light brown. Before I could come up with something to say, Miss Zora walked back into the room carrying a tray of salads.

"Your second course is now being served."

Like Shiloh, I wanted to offer my assistance too, but I took the lead from Miss Alaina and Miss Claudette and sat back and allowed Miss Zora to serve us. She really seemed to be getting a lot of pleasure from it.

"Your salads are simple heart of iceberg, topped with Maytag blue cheese dressing and crispy bacon bits.

I looked at the salad in front of me and marveled at the fact that it had never occurred to me that a quarter slice of iceberg lettuce could look so appetizing. Initially, I thought Ms. Zora was outdoing herself, by providing us with such a delicious meal, but then I remembered that she had lived and cooked in France, so our dinner was probably nothing compared to what she could really do. I looked up from my salad just as Shiloh looked up from his plate to look at me.

I quickly glanced over at Ms. Alaina, who was also looking at me. "Miss Shae, isn't this just fabulous? I bet you don't eat like this at school."

"Oh, no, absolutely not, our salads are at the

beginning of a buffet line, and usually it's just a bunch of cut up lettuce.

Shiloh wiped his mouth with his cloth napkin. "Where do you go to school, if you don't mind me asking?"

"I go to Miles College in Birmingham."

"That's cool. I've been up there with some of my boys. I go to Alabama State in Montgomery. You ever been there?

"No. Jemison is as about as far south of Birmingham as I've ever been."

"You should come down and visit sometimes."

Miss Claudette, who hadn't said much all day, looked up at him. "Shiloh, it would be nice of you to, maybe, take Miss Shae down there one weekend."

Miss Alaina was very pleased with Claudette's suggestion. "Ooh, Sister, there was nothing I liked better than a road trip when I was in college."

Before Shiloh or I could make a comment, Miss Zora walked in with the main course. "I can think of one thing you liked better, Sister, but we're in mixed company."

Miss Claudette and I laughed. Shiloh chuckled too. Surprisingly, Miss Alaina merely grinned to herself as she took a sip of her wine.

All of our attention quickly turned back to Miss Zora and the tray she was carrying.

Miss Claudette began to clap. "Oh, Sister, that looks delish. What is it?"

"It is Brenne Carp Fillets with St. Maure de Touraine Cheese or in French *filet de carpe de Brenne au Sait-*

Maure-de-Touraine, with mashed potatoes and chives; and steamed Jamaican cabbage. Well, the carp's not really from Brenne, but it is carp.

With that being said, we all began to clap, and, if I didn't know any better, it looked as if Miss Zora was blushing. It was really nice to see her being so playful, to see her so happy.

As we ate, you could hear a pin drop. Miss Zora had finally sat down to have dinner and, like everyone else, she was also enjoying the meal she prepared. The clink of the forks hitting the plate was almost musical. I discreetly glanced up to look at everyone else and, like before, Shiloh was looking at me. This time I didn't let it slide by.

"What?"

He kind of jumped, as if he was startled that I said something. "You have a little bit of cheese on your chin. I'll get it."

Before I could wipe my face with my napkin, Shiloh stood up and, reaching across the table, dabbed the trickle of cheese off of my chin.

"There, that's better."

"Thank you..." I blushed at his unsolicited attentiveness.

"Always such a gentleman, Shiloh," Miss Claudette smiled.

"Of course he is. He comes from good people, and just look him. If I was 30 years younger..."

"You'd still be old enough to be his mother." With that said, Miss Zora laughed and stood up, "Anybody else ready for dessert?"

We all laughed. This time Shiloh stood up and insisted that Miss Zora allow him to help her with the dishes. She handed him the tray, and then loaded it with all of our plates and silverware. Shiloh humbly followed her into the kitchen.

As soon as they cleared the door Miss Alaina came to life. "I've been biting my tongue all night. What do you think, Miss Shae?"

"About what?

"Oh, stop playing with me."

"I'm not. What do I think about what?"

"Girl, you know that boy is fine and he's a gentleman and he's smart and he's tall…shall I go on?"

I started laughing. "Yeah, he is all of that. He's nice."

Miss Alaina tried not to raise her voice. "Nice? Nice? That boy comes from good stock and he's a doggone good catch. Now, he's going to be a great husband one day." With her eyebrows raised, she crossed her arms and leaned on the table.

"Miss Alaina, you know I have a boyfriend…"

"Uh, huh…and nobody is suggesting that you stop dating him…tonight."

I turned to look at Miss Claudette. She merely looked back at me with her eyebrows also raised.

"What, Miss Claudette, you too?"

She smiled. "I didn't say anything, dear."

We then heard Miss Zora call from the kitchen. "Come on, we're going to have dessert on the back porch."

Miss Alaina, taking one last stab at me, pursed her lips and whispered, "Shiloh."

FOURTEEN

As we walked through the dark kitchen, Miss Alaina bumped into me and hollered out, "Sister, why'd you turn the damn lights off?"

Miss Claudette stopped in front of me, and then turned and put her finger up to her lips. "Sister, please. Don't ruin the evening. Zora is in such a good mood and we're having an absolutely lovely time with these young people. Please?"

"Well, why did she turn the lights off? She could have asked one of us to do that."

Miss Claudette cocked her head to one side and pleaded with her eyes.

The porch was also dark, except for the flickers of light strategically placed on the end tables. It was a warm evening and, though a slight breeze was blowing, the ceiling fan was on low.

"This was...a meeting of the minds, if you will." Miss Zora looked over at Shiloh and gave him a closed lip smile. "I wanted to serve dessert by candlelight in either the dining room or the parlor. You all can thank Mr. Shaw for suggesting that we have it out here on the porch, so that we could enjoy the evening breeze. He also reminded me that the fresh air would help with the digestion of our meal. How could I argue with that? So, here we are." She once again turned and smiled at Shiloh.

The flickers of yellow light made the blackness of Shiloh's skin shine golden as he stood in the middle of the porch holding a tray. "Ladies, if you would all have a seat, please. It would be my pleasure to serve your dessert."

Even by candlelight, dessert looked beautiful and uncomplicated. After such a wonderful dinner, I didn't know if I could eat another bite, but I wasn't willing to bypass dessert just because of that. I walked to the right, across the porch, and sat on a rattan loveseat. Miss Claudette and Miss Alaina followed behind me, but they both sat on the couch in front of the loveseat. As soon as we were comfortable, Shiloh began to serve us.

"Here you are, Miss Shae." He grinned as he said my name, showing all of his pearly whites. The silver and black bracelet on his right wrist reflected the moonlight.

"Thank you."

He then turned his attention to the couch, "And for you, Miss Claudette."

She smiled and bowed her head.

"And, of course, I would never forget you, Miss Alaina."

"Uh, huh…"

"Miss Zora…"

"Dear, you can take your dessert and be seated. Hand me the tray and I'll take it back into the kitchen, and then I can come right back out here to join everyone."

Shiloh took a serving of dessert off of the tray for himself and handed the tray to Miss Zora, as she had instructed. He then turned around, as if looking for a place to sit.

"Shiloh, it would probably be nice if Sister could sit in that chair you're standing next to – that way she doesn't have to walk across all of us when she comes back. Why don't you sit next to Miss Shae? Is that okay, Miss Shae?" Even in the soft light, you could see the mischievousness in Miss Alaina's eyes.

"Of course it is." I squinted at her as I spoke. It was painfully obvious what she was trying to do. She was relentless.

"Sit down, son, before Sister gets back out here.

Shiloh moved swiftly. "Yes, ma'am."

As he sat down, Miss Zora returned. "It's such a beautiful evening. It was a great night to have guests."

As she spoke, I put a spoonful of the lavender colored dessert into my mouth. "Oh, Miss Zora, what is this? Oh, my word, it…is…crazy…good!"

Everyone else tasted a spoonful of their dessert, as well, and from the chorus of mumbling, everyone agreed. Not only was the dish beautiful but it was equally as delicious.

Between each spoonful of his dessert, Shiloh

managed to offer his own compliment. "The only thing my mother and grandmother make that tastes anywhere close to this good is their peach cobbler, but don't tell them I said that."

Miss Zora beamed. "You young people are so kind. It's really nothing. It's a little dish I became acquainted with many years ago…in France. It's called Tulipes with Raspberry Sorbet."

I looked intently at Miss Zora. "This has got to be more than sorbet. Say it in French, please."

"Tulipe avec sorbet aux framboises."

Shiloh laughed. "That would explain why it tastes so good; it sounds really pretty, like everything else they say in French."

Our laughter broke through the quiet of the night.

"I'm going to tell my mother about this. Where can she buy it?"

"Oh, dear, I suppose I could make some for your family."

"You made this, Miss Zora?"

"Oh, yes, even the tulip bowl. That's the real treat; it's a cookie."

Even Miss Claudette stopped eating for a moment. "Sister, this is a real treat. You've never made this for me and Alaina. After all of these years, you never cease to amaze me. What looks so simple, a bowl of raspberry sorbet with a sprig of mint, is really something very special from your heart." Miss Claudette stood and kissed her sister on the cheek. "Thank you for sharing this with us and our young guests."

It seemed like Miss Zora was going to get emotional, but she remained stoic and offered to further serve us. "We've talked enough about food and what not. Would anyone like any coffee?"

"You can bring me another glass of wine, since I can't light a...."

Miss Zora stopped Miss Alaina. "I'll bring you the bottle." She then turned her attention to me and Shiloh. "Would either of you like anything else?"

Shiloh seemed to speak for both of us. "No, ma'am, everything was great tonight."

Miss Alaina interrupted him. "You're not leaving, are you? It's still early. Why don't you and Miss Shae go for a walk down by the lake while we clean up out here?"

Shiloh turned and looked at me. "You want to?"

I shrugged my shoulders. "Sure, why not?"

Miss Alaina clapped her hands and stood to her feet. "Well, now, good. You two go on and we'll be here when you get back."

Shiloh stood up, so I stood up too. He walked to the screen door and held it open. I walked passed him and down the stairs. We quietly walked next to each other across the yard to the path in the woods. I turned and looked back at the porch. I could see a new, small flicker of light. I was pretty sure Miss Alaina was lighting a joint. I smiled and shook my head.

It felt kind of strange that we were going on a walk with each other – two strangers – so I thought I should say something to break the monotony. "How long have you known the sisters?"

"They've been around here as long as I can remember, so I guess I've known them all of my life. Everybody in town knows them, though. They're sort of like celebrities around here."

"Yeah, that's the impression I got when I first arrived in town – that they were, like, celebrities or something. The sheriff tried to give me a really hard time," I laughed. "As a matter of fact, the first time I came here, he drove me out here to the house. That really tripped me out."

"Oh, yeah? I'm not surprised. He really brought you out here because he has a little thing for Miss Claudette."

"I thought so. I felt the vibe between them the first day. It was real cute."

"Okay, if you say so."

"What? Everybody deserves to have somebody. Speaking of which, where's your somebody?" I looked up at him as we approached the water porch.

He stopped and looked down at me. "I could ask you the same thing. Where's your somebody?"

"You first..."

Shiloh exhaled, "Well, I do have a girlfriend…"

"Of course you do."

"And you? How is it that you can spend the weekend here and leave your boyfriend back at Miles?"

I started walking again. "I'm, uhm…he plays on the basketball team."

"Athlete…huh, cool."

For some strange reason, I really wanted to explain

my relationship to him, to tell him that Shukree and I weren't serious or anything like that.

As we approached the water porch we could see all of the tiny, little, white lights all over the porch. As if it wasn't beautiful enough in the daylight, at night it was like something from a fairytale. I wasn't sure how I felt about being here...with Shiloh, though.

Shiloh looked down at me, and then back up at the porch. "It's really pretty, isn't it?"

I nodded my head. "Pretty is an understatement. I love it."

"Oh, I meant to say earlier, you look really cute in your outfit."

"Really?" I wrinkled my nose at him.

"Yeah, I really wanted to say something earlier, but I knew better than to do it in front of Miss Alaina. Could you imagine what the conversation during dinner would have been like if I had done that? She would have been crunk!" He put his hand on his forehead and blew air through his teeth. "You know Miss Alaina is out of control, right?"

I laughed. "Again, that's an understatement."

I walked up the stairs to the porch, as Shiloh walked behind me. The only thing on my mind was, *I wonder if he's looking at my booty? I hope not.* I didn't turn around to check, though. Instead, I walked over to one of the chairs that had the big, fluffy cushions and plopped down.

Shiloh swaggered over and sat down across from me. "So, how do you know the sisters?"

For the first time during the night, I realized he had on white Chuck Taylors. I also realized that he was even more handsome in the night light than he was during the day. How could that even be possible? I could see myself hanging out with him, but I don't know how we would work around the distance.

"Well, Shae, you never said how you know the sisters. You still with me or are you thinking about your boyfriend?"

"I heard you." I didn't realize my mind had wandered long enough for him to notice. "I'm taking classes this summer and in one of them I have to do a paper and, long story short, I chose to do it on them."

"Okay, that's cool. I mean, what's the paper about?"

"We have to write about somebody from a period in history and discuss how that period impacted their life. The sisters lived during the Harlem Renaissance, so after reading one of Miss Claudette's books I decided to do my paper on her and her sisters."

"How's it going?"

"Shiloh, do you really care?" I couldn't imagine that he did. I thought he was making small talk.

"No, really, I do care. I like them…a lot and I'm interested in hearing what you have to say."

I wasn't expecting that, especially the part about him being interested in my paper. I suppose he could be. What else did we have to talk about?

"Okay, if that's really what you want to talk about…"

He grinned. "Really, it's cool, even though I'd rather know more about you. Like, where you're from, uhm, you know, stuff like that."

I laughed because either he really wanted to know more about me or he was trying to finesse me. "Shiloh, I know that guys only pretend to want to know those things. What they're really doing is buying time, to figure out if they can 'get it on' with a girl."

"Get it on? Get it on? Who says that?" He laughed hard.

I liked the sound of his laughter.

"I'm glad you find me so funny."

I could barely speak without laughing at myself.

"I'll give you that one. I'm a guy. I like to 'get it on,' but you don't seem like the kind of girl that a guy can 'get it on' with on the first date. I think a guy would have to work really hard to take it to that level with you."

"It's not a date, but I'm going to take that as a compliment. You know what, though? Let's not go there."

"That's cool too." He looked at me for a few seconds then pointed at the little cabinet next to me. "I know for a fact, if you pull that drawer to your right open, there are cards and games, and stuff in there. You want to play cards or something, or do you just want to talk?"

I wasn't interested in playing cards, so we talked.

Eventually he looked down at his watch. "Miss Shae, I would love to sit out here with you and talk all night, but I have to go home and go to bed. It's, like, 1 o'clock in the morning."

"Really, we've been talking that long? Time flies in

good company."

"Yeah, it does." As he spoke he got up and walked over and sat next to me. "Miss Shae, honestly…for real, I have never done this before, but you have beautiful lips. I've been looking at them all night."

"So, that's what you were doing during dinner."

He nodded his head. "Yep, you have really pretty lips. Okay, so can I kiss you?"

I shrunk back from him a little. "What? Are you serious? Are you hitting on me?"

"No, Shae, I just want one kiss. I have never done this before, but, really, your lips are sexy as heck."

"Don't you have a girlfriend?"

"Yeah, and you have a boyfriend. I'm not asking you if I can 'get it on' with you," he chuckled. "I just want a kiss. And you know what?"

"What?"

"You haven't said no yet."

Well, he was right, I hadn't. I had never kissed anyone I had just met. I wanted to say no, but I couldn't because I was curious. I guess I was taking too long. With his right hand on my chin he steadied my face and kissed me.

I should have been angry that he would be so presumptuous, but I didn't pull away. I just went with it. Now I had to add 'good kisser' to the list of things I knew about Shiloh Manuell Shaw III.

When our lips parted, with his hand still on my chin, he sat back and we looked at each other for a couple of seconds before he spoke.

"Yeah...it's getting late. We better go."

FIFTEEN

Shiloh and I silently walked back to the house. I was surprised to find no one, as in Miss Alaina, waiting for us on the back porch. A nightlight had been put in the kitchen, so we quietly walked through the room then through the dining room and into the parlor, where Miss Claudette was sitting on the loveseat reading a book by the light of a table lamp.

She looked up at us and closed her book as we entered the room. "Well, I take it you two young people had a nice visit?"

Shiloh and I turned and looked at each other.

Shiloh smiled. "It was a great night, Miss Claudette. Dinner was great. The conversation was great. The company was great." He glanced back down at me.

I blushed.

"Well, like I was telling Shae, I have to get up early in the morning. So, I better go.

Miss Claudette put her book on the table and started

to get up.

"Oh, no, please, Miss Claudette. I'll walk Shiloh to the door…if that's okay?"

"Thank you, dear, I appreciate that. Good night, Shiloh."

"Good night, Miss Claudette. Please thank Miss Alaina and Miss Zora for me, and tell Miss Zora I'm going to tell my mother and grandmother about that tulip sorbet."

We all laughed.

I followed Shiloh out of the parlor to the front door. He opened the large red door and slowly walked out. Once we were actually standing on the porch, he turned back around to face me.

"So, when can I see you again?"

"When can you see me again? You have a girlfriend." I quickly turned around to see if Miss Claudette could hear me, before whispering, "I guess I'll be back in a couple of weeks."

He gave me a large, closed mouth grin. "Okay." Then he extended his hand.

I laughed and grabbed it.

"It was a pleasure meeting you, 'Miss Shae,' for real."

As he walked away he held onto my hand.

I laughed. "You have to let go."

"I don't want to, but, okay, if you say so." He pretended to make a sad face then he smiled and released my hand. As he was walking away he turned around. "When are you leaving?"

"Some time tomorrow evening, before dinner, I think."

"Okay. Good night."

"Good night."

I watched him as he walked to his car. I watched as he started his car and turned his car lights on. I watched as he backed up, and then turned around and drove down the long drive. I watched until the red lights on the back of his car disappeared into the darkness.

I finally closed the door and walked back to the parlor, where Miss Claudette was still sitting. She had started reading her book again. Once more she stopped, closed it, and looked up at me.

"I don't know about you, Miss Shae, but I'm going to call it a night."

"Me too, Miss Claudette."

I waited for her to turn off the lamp, and then I followed her up the stairs.

"Miss Claudette, tomorrow can we sit down after breakfast and start on the photo albums again?"

"Oh, yes, of course."

When we reached the top of the staircase Miss Claudette said good night without even turning around. I said good night to her and went to my room. I closed my bedroom door behind me and went to my duffle bag to pull out my pajamas. Before I could change into my sleepers there was a light knock at the door.

"Come in?"

It was Miss Alaina. She threw herself across the length of the bed like a teenager.

"Well?"

"Well, what?"

"That's cute. You always do that."

She was right. I only said that to buy time. I wanted to think about how I was going to respond to her questions, but it seemed like there were always so many, so fast.

"He's a really nice guy."

Miss Alaina rolled over on her back and laughed. "I hope y'all didn't have sex on the water porch because Sister would have a fit!"

I wrinkled my face up at her and shook my head. "Of course we didn't. Why would we do that? We don't even know each other."

"I always have sex on the first date if I really like the man I'm with. Always have. Always will...uh, huh."

I stood there and looked at her. I knew if I didn't tell her about the kiss she'd never leave the room and I wouldn't get any sleep. I closed my eyes and scratched my forehead.

"Shiloh kissed me..."

"Now you're talking! So y'all kissed out there. I knew it!"

"No, he kissed me."

"And you certainly didn't kiss him back; right? I mean, with his old, ugly, stinky self. His breath probably stank and everything." She laughed at her own joke.

I laughed so hard I had to cover my mouth with my hand. I shook my head at her and sat down on the bed next to her. When I did, she rolled over up against me.

"Well?"

By the way she raised her eyebrows and looked at me with her widely stretched eyes, I knew exactly what she wanted to know.

At that moment it wasn't even like I was talking to a 73 year old woman. It felt like I was talking with one of my girlfriends back at my apartment.

I leaned over close to her and whispered, "That boy can kiss like what!" I cut the air with my hand.

Miss Alaina sat up. "I knew it. I don't care what Sister says. If I was 30 years younger I would have taught him something by now."

With that said, she stood up to leave the room. Stopping in the doorway, she turned and looked back at me.

With a smile on her face, she held up two fingers very close in front of her face. "You're going to have two boyfriends, or one Shiloh Manuell Shaw."

Dropping one finger, she pointed at me as she left the room.

I jumped off the bed and quickly ran into the bathroom to take off my clothes. After getting dressed for bed, I grabbed my toothbrush to brush my teeth. When I came out of the bathroom I walked over to close the bedroom door and noticed a light on in Miss Zora's room. I was a little worried that something might be wrong, so I took a chance and slowly walked down the hallway. When I reached her door I stood there for a few seconds and listened, to see if I could hear anything. The truth was: I was a little afraid. She intimidated me much more than I let on. At first, I lightly tapped on the door, but I didn't hear anything. So, I knocked a little harder. I looked around to see if I had awakened either Miss Claudette or Miss Alaina, but there wasn't a sound coming from either of their rooms. When I turned back around to face Miss Zora's bedroom I thought I could hear her stirring around.

A barely audible sound came from the room. "Yes?"

I slowly opened the door and stuck my head in. "Are you okay, Miss Zora?"

I looked at her back as she sat on the side of her bed wearing a long, pink, silk gown. She slowly turned and looked at me.

"What are you still doing up, Miss Shae?"

"I was closing my bedroom door and I saw your light on. I thought, maybe, something was wrong."

She chuckled to herself. "Everything's fine. Sometimes I become a little parched in my sleep, so I get up in the middle of the night to get a glass of water."

"Oh, okay."

"Good night, again, Miss Shae."

"Good night." I started to pull her bedroom door closed, but then I pushed it back open. "Thank you for dinner tonight, Miss Zora. I really enjoyed everything."

She smiled. "It was my pleasure."

I smiled to myself and gently closed her bedroom door.

SIXTEEN

The next morning was uneventful, aside from breakfast and Miss Zora and Miss Claudette going to Sunday school at the local church. After they left, Miss Alaina and I sat on the back porch and talked, while she smoked her first joint of the day. After lighting it and taking a long pull, she held her breath and then turned her head away from me to exhale.

"You and Shiloh actually make a very cute couple, and please say something else other than 'I have a boyfriend.'" She rolled her eyes then sat and stared at me.

"Okay, I don't know Shiloh. We really just met last night."

Her forehead wrinkled. "So get to know him. How difficult could that be?"

I shook my head and looked up in the air. "You say that like it's really easy. I don't live here. I go to school in Birmingham and he goes to school in Montgomery, and I'm not driving back and forth just to see some guy, especially one that already has a girlfriend."

Miss Alaina chuckled. "You're silly." She then took a puff from her joint. "And you're making me waste some good weed. Look, you and he are not going to be in college forever and I doubt very seriously that either one of you is going to marry the person you're dating now. Why couldn't you meet up here in Jemison? Shiloh 'does' live here and there's nothing stopping either one of you from visiting here on weekends; right?"

I shook my head from side to side.

"Oh, that's right, *you have a boyfriend*. Child, please, why are you dating him anyway? You haven't said more than five words about this boyfriend either time that you've visited us. I'm not crazy. I know that means much more than you're telling us. You're not just here to do a class project. You're also here because you're trying to get away from him. Tell the truth. You don't really want to be with him, do you? How long have you been dating him, what's his name, Shuckee?" She turned her head and put her tiny cigarette back up to her lips.

Her words stung a little bit. I guess that was because she was right. I get tired of Shukree always lying, even though I'm only dating him for my own selfish reason: so I don't have to be bothered with any other guys on campus, but it's not like I don't like him because I do. It would be crazy to date someone I don't even like. And, actually, we do have fun together. It's just that...

"Miss Lady!" Miss Alaina snapped her fingers. "You don't know how long you've been dating him either, huh?"

I looked at her and smiled. "His name is Shukree and we've been dating since the end of my sophomore year. So, almost two years."

Miss Alaina fanned her hand in the air. "He's just your college boyfriend. You all aren't going to get married and now would be as good a time as any to make a clean break and start dating Shiloh. He's smart, good looking, hardworking, and he comes from good people, and he's marriage material. And that means something because all men are not marriage material. That's one thing I know for sure."

For the first time since I had met her, she sounded like she was really serious. I don't know why Shiloh and I getting together is so important to her, but it seemed to be. I didn't want to talk about it anymore though.

"Why didn't you ever get married?"

Miss Alaina coughed into her hand and then smiled at me. "I almost got married one time. His name is Gollie."

"What kind of name is that," I chuckled.

"Of course, that's not his real name. That's just what everyone called him. His real name is William Langston Burroughs III. He told me that when he was a very little boy he was extremely inquisitive and asked lots of questions, but he always started the question off with, 'Gol-lee, what's that or gol-lee, why did they do that,' so his family started calling him Gol-lee, and as the years went on the nickname stuck and it gradually became Gollie. It was appropriate for another reason too. He was so black and good looking that when the girls saw him they said, 'Gol-lee, did you see him? As a matter of fact, I think I said it, too, the first time I saw him." She put her hand over her mouth and laughed. "He was also very athletic. I think he excelled at everything he did, including women."

"Is that why you didn't marry him?"

"Honestly, it wasn't that simple. I dated a lot too, you know. Remember, I told you that in one of our previous conversations. Gollie was different, though. I fell in love with him. He apparently fell in love with me too. It was the only time in my life that 'I' was the one that wanted a monogamous, mutually exclusive relationship. I had dated plenty of guys that wanted an exclusive relationship with me, but I just wasn't interested in having a relationship with them like that, for one reason or another. Sister Zora would say it was because I was too selfish and that I used the men for what I could get from them: sex, money, dates, trips, whatever, but, you know, that just wasn't true. None of them had what Gollie had. I think, maybe, he was the male version of me." She smiled, looked down at her hands, and then looked up out at the backyard.

"Gollie didn't ask me to change a single thing about myself. A lot of the other guys wanted me to be more ladylike or they wanted me to slow down because I was always involved in social and political activities. I don't regret any of the time I spent doing things like marching for civil rights or working on voter's rights for black folks because there were times when there needed to be a voice for the people, and I was more than glad to be that voice. Gollie actually liked that about me. Hmph! Our pillow talk was often about what we could do to help our community. He actually supported my social and political ideologies because his were pretty similar. I think that's what made me fall in love with him. He was never afraid that my mouth might get me into trouble with white folks. He wasn't afraid of anything. When we were together we worked hard, we laughed hard, we played hard, and we loved hard. For me, he was the complete package."

Miss Alaina swallowed and sat quietly in her seat. The fire on the tiny cigarette in between her fingers had long ago gone out, as her hand lie in her lap supported around the wrist by her other hand. She looked neither happy nor sad as she reminisced. For a minute, I thought she had forgotten that I was sitting there.

"He asked me to marry him, but after I met his parents, who were both in the medical profession, his father was a doctor and his mother was a nurse. You know, it was the one time when I cared what someone thought about me. I never got the feeling that they liked me. I think they were both very genteel people, but I don't think I was quite what they wanted for their son. Gollie never told me that, though. Oh, and his parents were always extremely kind to me, but there was always something in their eyes when they looked at me. Something that made me question whether or not I needed to change to accommodate *their* desires for *their* son, and I think I might have – changed, that is – because I loved Gollie that much." Tears pooled in her eyes, but she didn't cry.

I, on the other hand, felt a tear run down my own cheek. Miss Alaina and Ms. Zora shared one thing in common: they both had experienced and lost the one true love in the lives. I sat silently and continued to listen.

Miss Alaina turned and looked at me. A smile spread across her face as she reached up and wiped the one lone tear from my cheek. "You know, in spite of what they may have thought about me, Gollie was no saint either. Every kind of woman alive at the time was drawn to him – short, tall, black, white, Asian, old, young – and he was more than obliged to charm them, all of them. Well, most of them. Women younger than him were off limits. Back then it could have been a death sentence for a black man to have relations with a white woman. It could have meant death if he was caught or even accused of flirting with one. So, if he had any dealings with them he was extremely discreet about it.

I couldn't keep up with the women, though, and, yes, believe it or not, it became a point of contention for us. Though, Gollie always assured me that I had absolutely nothing to worry about because his dealings with other women wasn't what I thought it was. He never referred to those associations as relationships. In his words, 'Laina, you're the only woman in my life that I have ever had a serious relationship with.' He assured me that he was in love with me and only me. And you know what? I believed him. I wasn't worried that I would lose him to any one of them. Yet, I was concerned because there always seemed to be so many of them. I mean, after all, we were engaged to be married. I had stopped seeing other men, so I didn't think it was too much to expect him to stop spending time with other women too. I might have been a little wild back then, but I was intelligent and practical. I understood that it would take some time for him to stop seeing the other women and even then I had no reason to believe that his behavior would immediately change upon us jumping the broom. For the first and only time in my life I felt jealous.

So, dealing with that and what his parents thought of me became too much for me. Like I said, after meeting his parents, I was willing to change because I loved Gollie, but at what cost? To this day, I can honestly say that I have never run from anything or anybody...except for William Langston Burroughs III. And, if you're wondering, let me assure you, I did not run from love. I've thought about it a lot over these many years and I eventually came to the conclusion that I ran from all of the changes that I would have had to make to accommodate my love for Gollie. If we had gotten married, I don't think I could have remained the person he fell in love with. Though, I do believe that love requires some give and take, some compromise, if you will, I would have had to do much more than just compromise."

"So, you never fell in love again?"

Miss Alaina stood and looked down at me as she put her tiny cigarette in her pocket. "My dear, I've never fallen out of love."

SEVENTEEN

As we made our way from the backyard to the front of the house to meet Miss Claudette and Miss Zora, Miss Alaina slid her arm through mine and we walked arm in arm.

"Miss Shae, there are only few regrets in life. One of them is not being with the person that you love. And, you know, it's quite possible that during a person's lifetime they might fall in and out of love a few times, but when you actually find someone that you love, that loves you back just right, and I'm not talking about sex either, you have to hold on tight," her fists involuntarily clenched as she spoke. "I hope you don't feel like I'm pressuring you to be with Shiloh," she paused. "Even though, the truth is, I might be, a little bit. I have known that young man since before he was born. I have always wished and prayed that life would be kind to him. That

141

included him finding someone that would solidly love and support him. It's difficult for young black boys and it gets more difficult for them as they become men, so having a good, supportive woman by their side means more than this world would have you to believe." She stopped walking and turned to face me. Grasping both of my hands she continued. "My sisters and I have always been good judges of character, and the fact that you sit and listen to our stories, the fact that you even chose to come spend your time with three elderly women says a lot about who you are. We have never been wrong about anyone. Not anyone. After you left last week, Zora even said it was too bad that you and Shiloh didn't go to the same school because you both had the same kind of *spirits*. Both you and he have an affinity for older people that would be considered outstanding in this day and time when young people are so disrespectful.

I have to tell you, I don't know how much it should mean to either of you, but even Zora thinks you and Shiloh would make a good couple. She would never say anything to either of you about it, though. I, on the other hand…," she laughed. "I can't leave it to chance. I think both of you need a little bit of gentle nudging."

"Miss Alaina, I would be a liar if I said I wasn't attracted to him. Shoot, I've been attracted to him ever since the first time I saw him cutting the grass. I mean, but, there are so many things going on…"

"You have a boyfriend. I know."

"Well, yeah, that too, but, you know, being a virgin, it's not like I can date all of these guys and just expect

142

them to respect that. They always seem to want that from you – sex, I mean. I've worked it out with Shukree so that he doesn't pressure me. Every now and then he asks, but I say no and we move on pass it."

Intertwining her arm with mine, Miss Alaina began to walk again. "Trust me, given the chance, he would be on you like white on rice. Of course, you know he's having sex with other girls, right?"

I exhaled hard. "Yeah, I know."

"That's why I'm sure your relationship with him won't last beyond college. You have integrity. He doesn't. Some would say he's just being a guy. You understand, he doesn't have another girlfriend; he's merely having sex with these other girls. I'm sure he feels like none of that has anything to do with the relationship he has with you. At least he shelters you from all of the drama that could ensue from these other young women. That says something about him. I suppose. I haven't known you long, but I think I know you well enough to say you wouldn't marry someone like that – someone that so liberally has sex with other people. Having sex with other people means so little to him and so much more to you, right? In spite of how different you and I are from each other, I guess you and I still share something in common, huh? The only difference is you're not in love with Shukree."

As we came from around the house we could see a cloud of dust behind the teal Mercedes as it slowly came down the long, dirt driveway. Ms. Claudette was at the wheel.

Miss Alaina stopped next to the porch. Smiling, she waved at her sisters as if they were returning from a long trip. "Please don't mention our conversation about Gollie and Shiloh to my sisters. Zora wouldn't be pleased with either. She would reprimand me for talking about Shiloh and she was never fond of Gollie, so knowing that we spent the entire morning talking about them would displease her."

I looked over at her and smiled. "Of course not, I appreciate our private time together this morning."

I studied the side of her face. Her skin was beautiful. Not one single wrinkle. Now that I thought about it, none of them had any wrinkles. None of them had fully grey hair either. Miss Alaina's hair was salt and peppered, but Miss Claudette and Miss Zora had not a hint of grey on either of their heads. I continued to smile to myself as the Mercedes came to a stop in front of us.

I walked over to open Miss Zora's door as Miss Alaina opened Miss Claudette's.

Miss Zora had barely put a foot on the ground when she began with her repartee. "Sister, I hope you didn't corrupt Miss Shae while we were away." Her smile indicated she was being playful.

Miss Alaina laughed and pointed at me. "Ask her what we talked about. We spent the entire time talking about sex and drugs! Well, not drugs, just marijuana." Laughing, she helped Miss Claudette out of the car.

Miss Claudette shook her head and smiled. "What are

we going to do with you, Alaina?"

"Love me." Miss Alaina kissed her on the cheek as she grabbed her hand before walking in my direction.

Miss Claudette closed her eyes and accepted her sister's affection. "Well, I don't know about you ladies, but I could use a little snack. We ate quite early this morning."

"Because it's such a beautiful day, after I change clothes, let's have brunch on the back porch. I'll quickly whip up something for us to eat." Miss Zora bounced up the steps without looking back. Once she reached the beautiful, red door she held the doorknob and turned back around. She spoke into the air, as if thinking aloud. "Maybe we can have brunch out on the water. Yes, that would be a great idea."

Standing in between me and Miss Claudette, Miss Alaina ran her arms under ours and held tight as we walked toward the stairs.

As we topped the first step, Miss Claudette stopped and looked over at me. "Did sister get a chance to tell you about our annual end of the summer barbecue?"

"No, ma'am, she didn't mention it."

"We talked about so much. How could I have forgotten about that?" Miss Alaina turned and winked at me.

EIGHTEEN

We pushed lunch to the water porch on two, beautiful, wooden carts with wheels. I wasn't surprised that Miss Zora had carts especially made for serving food. It was also no surprise that our brunch was another uniquely different meal from any of the other meals I had already had the pleasure of eating with them.

As Miss Zora served our after dinner tea, hot papaya, mango, green tea, she beamed as they continued to tell me about their annual barbecue.

"So you cook all of the food, Miss Zora?"

"Well, not actually. I prepare all of the meats, several side dishes and salads, as well as a few desserts, but the community is welcome to bring one additional side dish, salad, or dessert per family, and they also provide all of the ice and drinks."

"Sister's food is ready and perfectly presented, buffet style, on several tables by the time everyone arrives. That is, with the exception of the fried fish, of course.

Everyone knows you can't begin frying the fish until after the first guests arrive. And you better believe the oil is hot, ready, and waiting." Miss Claudette looked over at Miss Zora and gave her an approving nod.

"It sounds like a really big deal."

"It is. Everyone from Jemison comes. You should bring your friends from school." Mischievousness was written all over Miss Alaina's face as she sipped from her tea."

"I will. They'll be glad to come. It means free food."

Everyone laughed as the conversation slowly transitioned back to my project. Miss Zora eventually excused herself to take her afternoon nap, so we pushed the carts back to the house. Though I knew she wouldn't allow me to help her in the kitchen, I offered my assistance anyway. Even Miss Claudette and Miss Alaina seemed tired, so I thought it was a good time to get on the road back to Birmingham.

"Girl, I don't know if I want to go to some picnic at some house way out in the country. Will there be any guys there?"

"Melodi, stop trippin'! It'll be good for you to get away from here for a day, and plus you can see what you're going to be like when you get older." I laughed as I unpacked my dirty clothes and put them in the hamper.

Following me into my bedroom, Melodi plopped down on my bed and rolled over onto her back. "What do you mean by that? One of those old ladies reminds you of me?"

I rolled my eyes and answered without turning to look at her. "Uh, huh, she still likes to have sex and she smokes weed."

"Uhhh…I don't even want to hear about nobody as old as my grandparents having sex, and you never told me they smoked weed."

"No, just one of them, Miss Alaina. She's real cool. You'll like her a lot. She says whatever comes to mind and, yes, she still smokes weed. She told me she has been smoking since college and she didn't see any reason why she should stop now. From what she told me, she was wild when she was in college." I stopped and threw a dirty pair of jeans at Melodi. "Sort of like you!"

"That's nasty! Don't be throwin' your stank clothes at me."

Tossing the jeans back at me, I caught them in mid-air and threw them into the hamper. We laughed and walked back into the living room to watch TV.

"So, are you going to invite Shukree?"

Holding the remote control in my hand, I blindly flipped through the stations. "Of course, why wouldn't I?"

"Are we all going to ride together?"

I stopped and looked at her. "Yeah, why wouldn't we?"

"I don't know. I just thought I would ask. Anyway, what's up with Shukree tonight? Does he know you're back? Oh, my bad. Maybe he's busy." Twisting her lips, she lifted herself onto a side chair and folded her legs underneath her Indian style. "What, you're not going to say anything?"

"What do you want me to say, Melodi?" I turned my back to her.

It seems like everybody is more concerned about my relationship with Shukree than I am. I'm glad he hasn't called, though. Maybe we've played out and he's moved on. Would my feelings be hurt? I don't think I know the answer to that...yet. I do know what the answer isn't – Shiloh. Smiling to myself, I started flipping through the channels again.

"Turn to something funny. And I'm sorry. I shouldn't have asked you that. You know I'm just trippin'; right?"

"It's okay, we're cool." I sat down and put the remote control on the table next to me.

The phone rang, startling both of us.

"You want me to go get that?"

Frowning, I side-eyed her and shook my head. "Let the answering machine get it."

"Whaaat? Oooh, you know who it is; right?" Melodi took the throw on the back of her chair and put it over her shoulders as she repositioned herself in her chair.

"I'll see him tomorrow."

"Tomorrow? Uh, huh, I know, and don't forget to tell him that we're going on a road-trip together. I'm sure he's going to be really excited to hear that."

NINETEEN

"So tell me again, why are we going to some old lady's house? Is this part of your project, too?"

"Like I told you a hundred times already, Shukree, it's a picnic – free food, music, nice people, free food – remember?" I kept my attention focused on the road to keep from rolling my eyes at him.

Melodi stuck her head in between the front seats from the back seat. "You never really told me if there were going to be any single guys there." She turned and smiled at Shukree then quickly turned her attention back to me.

Shukree laughed, "No reason for Shae to know that. She's bringin' her man with her." Turning the volume knob on the radio, Shukree rocked to the music blaring from the speakers. "Right, Shae?"

"Boy, ain't nobody talkin' about for Shae! You so silly. Everybody knows you're her boyfriend, 'SHUKREE'! And turn the music down so I can talk."

Turning the back of head to Shukree, Melodi looked at me with one of her eyebrows raised up. "So, 'Shae,' guys, music, food at this picnic, right?"

"Yep, right."

Melodi sat back in her seat, but not before turning and licking her tongue out at Shukree.

We were the first to arrive, so I parked in the shade of one of the trees that lined the dusty driveway. As Melodi walked on my right and Shukree walked on my left, Shukree grabbed my hand and lifted it to his lips and kissed it.

Melodi, looking Shukree up and down, wrinkled her nose, "Who you tryin' to impress? You need to stop trippin', for real."

"Look, neither one of y'all better not embarrass me today. Seriously, I'm not playing with either one of y'all."

"Girl, ain't nobody gonna embarrass you. I'm not even thinkin' about her."

Melodi looked up and saw someone open the big, red door. Whispering, she smiled, "One of your friends is at the door, Shae." Talking through her teeth, Melodi quickly leaned forward and looked at Shukree. "And good, you don't have any business thinkin' about me!"

Just in time, right before Shukree and Melodi could start an argument, Miss Alaina stood at the top of the steps of the porch. I saw her glance at Shukree's hand still holding mine.

"Well, hello, I'm Alaina Lee Roberts. This must be Shukree." She extended her hand."

"Yes, ma'am."

"Cute and a strong handshake, too, I like that. It's nice to finally meet the boyfriend. I've heard so much about you."

"Thank you, it's nice to meet you too." Shukree turned and looked at me.

Taking a step back, Miss Alaina put her finger on her chin and looked Melodi up and down, from head to toe. "And this cute little thing must be the best friend, Melodi. I already think I like you. It's very nice to meet you, as well."

Melodi stepped onto the porch and gave Miss Alaina a tight hug then stepped back and looked her up and down. "Miss Alaina, it's my pleasure to finally meet you. You're not only beautiful, you're sassy!"

Miss Alaina threw her arm across Melodi's shoulders and began walking towards the door. "Thank you. I know." She smiled and squeezed Melodi as they both laughed at their private joke. "Come on, let me take you all into the house to introduce you to my sisters. As you can tell, you're the first to arrive. I'm glad, though. It'll give us all a little time to warm up to each other before everything gets started.

I don't know why, but I was surprised at how helpful Shukree was proving to be. Not so surprised about Melodi, though. She and Miss Alaina had hit it off and were spending a lot of time whispering and laughing like they were best friends – vexing Miss Zora. I could tell because she repeatedly cut her eyes at them. I knew Miss Zora had to be thinking Miss Alaina was corrupting Melodi. That was funny because Melodi could probably corrupt Miss Alaina. It would be mutual corruption.

As people began arriving, including Sheriff Granger, the atmosphere became livelier. Everyone that arrived was happy and excited, especially the children, because an area of the backyard had been partitioned off as a pretty impressive play area for them.

Miss Zora called me over to where she was frying fish. "Miss Shae, would you run into the house and grab another one of these large aluminum pans for me, please?" She pointed to a pan full of fish on the table next to her.

"Yes, ma'am, of course."

As I turned to walk across the yard, I saw a group of people coming through the gate – two women carrying covered dishes, an older man pulling a large cooler, another man carrying cases of soda, and Shiloh talking with a younger woman as he carried two bags of ice. My heart literally skipped a beat. My eyes followed the group across the yard until it occurred to me that I was supposed to be doing something for Miss Zora. Before hurrying to the kitchen, I quickly looked around to see if anyone was watching me. Standing in the doorway of the back porch were Melodi and Miss Alaina, whispering.

"Excuse me."

Melodi stepped to one side. "What's wrong with you?"

"Nothing's wrong with me." After walking passed both of them I realized they hadn't seen me watching Shiloh, so I quickly walked into the kitchen to grab an aluminum pan off of the counter. Pushing my way between the newfound friends, I headed back outside. "Why don't y'all come outside and socialize with everybody?"

Miss Alaina, leaning up against the door jam, put her hand on her hip. "Since when did you start telling me what to do, Miss Shae?" Intertwining her arm with Melodi's, she pulled her up against her side. "I think you're mad because I've made a new friend. Me-lo-di can be my friend, too," she laughed.

"Miss Alaina, you know better than all of that."

They smiled at each other then turned and smiled at me.

"I know y'all haven't been smok…"

Playfully pouting, Miss Alaina continued. "What?" Laughing she released Melodi's arm. "Uh, huh, friend, let's go 'socialize' like Miss Shae told us to."

Looking back, Melodi hopped down the steps in front of me. "I'm hungry anyway."

I watched as she and Miss Alaina disappeared into the crowd of people in the backyard. As I made my way back over to Miss Zora with the pan she had earlier asked for, I looked up just in time to see Shiloh's head turn away. He had been watching me.

TWENTY

After the last pan of fish was fried, Miss Zora handed it to me. "Would you be so kind as to take this over to the table? I think that's it. What do you think?"

"I think you're right. And anyway, you've been on your feet for a couple of hours, so I know you're tired. Why don't you go in the house to get some rest? I'll be glad to bring a plate in to you."

Before Miss Zora could respond, Shiloh walked over with the young woman that arrived with him and his family.

"Miss Alaina, I'll be glad to take that fish, if you'd like."

"Well, thank you, Shiloh. That's very kind of you."

Shiloh then turned his attention to me. "I'll take that, if you want me to, Shae." He paused just long enough for us to quickly look into each other's eyes. "There's been so much going on that I hadn't gotten a chance to introduce you to my girlfriend, Ciarra. Ciarra, this is Shae. She's the one that I told you had been visiting the Roberts sisters this summer, for a class project."

I felt a knot in my stomach. Why had he been talking to his girlfriend about me? She was pretty, just like I thought she would be. Smiling, I handed Shiloh the pan of hot fish. "Thanks, Shiloh, and it's nice to meet you, Ciarra."

Extending her hand, she returned the smile. "It's nice to meet you, too, Shae. Shiloh told me about your paper. It's a great idea – don't know how or when, but it made me think that I might want to steal the idea from you." She smiled.

After wiping my hands on the apron that Miss Zora had insisted I wear, I shook her hand. "That would be cool with me."

"You young people still have the energy that I wish I had. I'm going into the house to get cleaned up then I'm going to get a little rest, so that I can come back out and enjoy everyone. Good to see you again, Ciarra, and thank you again, Shiloh."

For a few seconds the three of us stood and watched Miss Zora as she walked towards the back porch.

Stretching his eyes wide, Shiloh lifted the pan up. "I better get this over to the table. You know how folks feel about hot, fried fish."

I nodded my head. "That's a good idea." Smiling, I glanced over at Ciarra, who had never moved from Shiloh's side. "Like I said, it's nice to meet you, Ciarra. Maybe I'll see you at the dessert table or on the dance floor." I didn't know what else to say.

Laughing, Melodi fell up against me and hugged me after the electric slide. "Shukree, how did I not know you could dance with your big, ole', tall self? Shae, girl, he can almost out dance you."

Laughing, Shukree pushed her shoulder. "You need to hang out with me and my boys sometimes. Shae knows what's up. Right, Shae?"

"I might just do that now that I know you have mad skills on the dance floor."

As we sat back down at our table, our laughter blended in with the rest of the laughter and talking in the backyard. Looking around, I saw that Miss Alaina was still on the dance floor. Earlier I had seen Miss Claudette and Sheriff Granger walking on the path leading to the water porch. I hadn't seen Miss Zora since she finished with the fish.

"Hey, I'll be right back. I'm going to go check on Miss Zora." I knew she was probably fine, but I had offered to bring her something to eat. "Do y'all need anything while I'm up?"

Melodi put both of her hands on her stomach. "I can't eat another bite. I might get up and dance a little more with Miss Alaina, so that I can make room for dessert later, though."

"Okay, what about you, Shukree?"

Grabbing my hand, Shukree pulled me close to him.

"Yeah, you can bring me something to drink."

My eyes nervously scanned the yard to see if Shiloh was watching. "Okay, boy, but you got'ta let me go." I playfully pushed away from him.

Shukree swung to smack me on the butt, but he missed and hit the side of my thigh. "Shae, thanks for making me come with you. I'm really having a good time."

"Of course you are. I'll be right back."

I don't know why it mattered if Shiloh saw us together because he was with his girlfriend and he and I hadn't said more than two words to each other all day, if you don't count when he introduced me to her, but I didn't want Shiloh to see me and Shukree hugged up together. Nor did I want to see him hugged up with Ciarra.

The house was quiet, so I walked up the stairs to see if Miss Zora was in her bedroom. As I reached the second floor I heard the back door shut. I turned to find Shiloh coming up the steps, two at a time.

"Boy, where are you going?"

When he reached the top step he stopped in front of me. Looking down, he wrapped his arms around me, and kissed me. As if on cue, I clutched the back of his t-shirt.

When our lips parted I stepped back and whispered, "Are you crazy? What if somebody sees us?"

"I've wanted to do that ever since I got here." Turning away from me, he took the stairs two at a time as he went back down to the ground floor.

When he reached the bottom he turned and looked up

at me. We silently stared at each other for a few seconds before he turned to leave the house through the front door. Now I was more confused than ever. I crossed my arms across my stomach and watched the front door. I suppose I was waiting for Shiloh to come back and explain what had just happened, but he never did, so I walked over to Miss Zora's bedroom door and knocked.

TWENTY-ONE

"Thanks for staying and cleaning up. That was really nice of y'all."

Melodi leaned forward through the front seats from the backseat. "For real, Shae? You act like we don't have any home training." She turned and looked at Shukree then turned back and looked at me. "Why wouldn't we stay and help? I ate so much I felt like I was obligated to help do something, and I'm not even going to talk about how much food we're bringing back with us." Laughing, she fell back into her seat.

"Man, I had a good time!" Shukree reclined his seat as he spoke. "And what's up with Miss Alaina? First I thought I smelled weed on her then I thought she was trying to hit on me."

Melodi and I burst out laughing.

"No, for real, what's up with her?"

"Melodi kicked her barefoot between the seats and put her foot on Shukree's arm. "So you sayin' you wouldn't get with that?"

I cracked up because that was pretty funny, when you thought about how Shukree is.

"Girl, you crazy, and get your foot off me!" Grabbing her foot, he squeezed it before pushing her leg back into the backseat.

"Seriously, though, what's up with 'Shiii-lowww'?"

I glanced up at the rearview mirror to find Melodi looking at me.

"Dude was there with his girl. I thought you said you was lookin' for single dudes?" Shukree was laid back in his seat with his arms across his eyes. "What he want with you? Old girl was hot."

I glanced over at him, and then looked back up at the rearview mirror. Melodi was still looking at me.

"What do you mean, what's up with him? Uhh…he goes to Alabama State. He's from Jemison. He cuts their grass." I maintained eye contact with her as I spoke.

"He's fine, ain't he – with his triple-chocolate self." She puckered up her lips and winked at me.

I was still looking at her when Shukree grabbed my knee and squeezed it. "I thought I saw him checkin' you out one time, though."

"Yeah?" I glanced up at the rearview mirror, but quickly turned my attention back to the road.

"But you got'ta man, so I wasn't even fazed. He needs to keep his eyes on that hottie he got."

I side-eyed him, "Yep, you're right. I have a man."

"That's what I'm talkin' 'bout, baby." Turning towards me, he kissed in the air.

Once we arrived back in Birmingham, we split the food with Shukree in the parking lot before I gave him a quick kiss on the lips and said goodnight. Melodi and I went into the apartment with our groceries that, for sure, would last for more than a week. In spite of all of the food we ate at the picnic, after putting our food away, Melodi and I heated up our plates in the microwave and settled down in the living room to eat again, or so I thought.

"So, for real, Shae, girl, what's up with you and Shiloh?" She kept her eyes on me as she picked up some barbecue chicken with her fingers and put it in her mouth.

"Psss, ain't nothin' goin' on with me and that boy. What did Miss Alaina tell you?"

"Shae, it's me. Come on now, my girl ain't say nothin' to me about nothin'. I saw him checkin' you out too." Frowning, Melodi seemed to focus more on the plate in her lap. With her mouth full, she looked up at me with her eyebrows raised. "And I saw how you looked at him too."

Raising my fork to my lips, I stopped short of putting the food in my mouth. "He was checkin' me out? When?"

"Whenever he could, but that's beside the point. I wouldn't be mad at you. I mean, for real, you and Shukree ain't going nowhere – not for real. I don't know much about Shiloh, except that Miss Alaina really likes him a lot and she thinks y'all would make a good couple."

I thought long and hard about what I wanted to say next. Melodi is my best friend and she knows me better than anybody. I just don't want her to argue with Shukree and slip and say something that I told her. She never has before, but this was different.

I swallowed the food in my mouth and looked up at her. "Shiloh and I kissed."

Melodi put her fork on her plate and hurriedly wiped her hand on the napkin in her lap. Moving to the edge of her chair, she stood up then quickly sat back down.

"That's what I'm talkin' 'bout. I knew somethin' was up with y'all. I didn't think it was that, but I knew somethin' was up. I can't believe you been holdin' out on me. So, what happened?"

"They invited him over for dinner one weekend while I was there and after dinner we went out to the water and talked. Before we came back to the house he kissed me."

Shaking her head from side to side, Melodi scooted back in her chair with her plate on her lap. "Dude, you have to get with Shiloh. Not, like, just get with him. I mean, like, cut Shukree loose and be with Shiloh. He is so much better than Shukree – so much better. So what you gon' do?"

"Okay, Miss Alaina. I have a boyfriend and, as you saw, Shiloh has a girlfriend." I stood up to take my plate to the kitchen.

Laughing, Melodi followed behind me. "You can call me what you want, plus she real cool people, so I ain't even mad about that, but, no, really, Shae." Exhaling, she put her plate on the kitchen counter and crossed her arms over her stomach. "Serious talk, so look, Shae, no matter what, somebody is going to get hurt. It's either going to be now or later. It's either going to be you or Shukree. Don't act like you don't know what's up."

Leaning back against the counter across from her, I looked at her. "So what about Ciarr—"

Melodi put her hands up over her ears. "Why do you keep talkin' about the girlfriend? You don't know her, so you don't owe her anything. And anyway...," Melodi took a couple of steps across the kitchen then grabbed me by my shoulders and shook me. "...if Shiloh was so into her why did he kiss you?"

She had a point. "He kissed me today too."

Melodi released me and paced through the kitchen. "What, are you serious? Girl, you are killin' me. When? How? You ain't nobody's friend. You be holdin' out!"

"He came in behind me, when I went in the house to get Miss Zora, and came upstairs and kissed me." I grabbed my plate then hers and scraped the scraps from both of them into the garbage can before rinsing them and putting them in the dishwasher.

"Who are you? I don't even know you anymore." Melodi laughed as we walked back into the living room. "You came out of that house with Miss Zora like nothin' had happened. I believe you the player. Shukree sittin' right outside and you in the house kissin' somebody else."

"Girl, shut up. You're crazy. It wasn't like that." I grabbed the remote and flipped through the channels as she went on.

"Serious talk, again, so what are you going to do, keep going on like this and end up having a secret relationship with Shiloh, which I know you're not going to do, or are you going to end it with Shukree and get with Shiloh? Like I said earlier, either way, feelings are going to get hurt. It's unavoidable."

I placed the remote on my lap. "Melodi, I go to school in Birmingham and he goes to school in Montgomery. That's another thing. I'm not trying to ride up and down the road for a guy. You know what? I don't even want to talk about this anymore. I'm going to take a shower and go to bed." Standing up, I handed her the remote control.

"I bet he would drive to Birmingham for you." She pointed the remote control at me as she spoke.

I stopped briefly, but thought it might be better to just go on into my bedroom. "Goodnight, Melodi."

"Goodnight, player, player."

TWENTY-TWO

"I've thoroughly enjoyed everyone's journals for this project, which, I remind you, is going to be seventy-five percent of your total grade for the semester. I'm really interested to see how you pull these composite reports together into the final paper." Professor Snead turned and winked at me as he walked back to the front of the class.

After, maybe, my second visit to Jemison it no longer felt like I was visiting for a class assignment. It felt more like I was visiting family. I had grown accustomed to all of the Roberts sisters' ways, even Miss Zora. It was hard to believe that the semester was almost over. Shukree was really busy traveling for actual games, no more preseason, scrimmage games, so we didn't see each other in the evenings that often. We tried to have lunch together every day that he was on campus and we talked on the phone, as much as possible. I hated to admit it, but that was more than enough for me.

Melodi was still in my ear about Shiloh, but I hadn't seen him since the picnic. A couple of times I tried to nonchalantly ask Miss Claudette about him, but she said they hadn't seen much of him either. Since the weather had changed, there wasn't much of a need for him to come by the house to cut the grass. I'm sure they knew how to get in contact with him, but I knew I couldn't dare ask for his phone number without Miss Alaina making a big deal out of it. The truth is that it is a big deal, but I'm just going to leave it alone. As I was lost in thought, Shukree walked up behind me, startling me.

Kissing me on my neck, he wrapped his arms around my waist. "Hey, beautiful! Girl, I miss you. What do you want to do for lunch?"

"Boy, you better say your name when you grab me from behind like that," I playfully teased with him.

Picking me up off my feet, Shukree whispered in my ear, "I know better than that. Every dude on this campus knows I'll bust him up if they even try to hit on you."

Oh, all this time I thought they stayed away from me because they respected the basketball star Shukree Jones, but it's because you've threatened everybody. Boy, you play too much."

When he put me down I turned to face him. "Do you have time to go off campus for Chinese food?"

Smiling, Shukree kissed me on the lips, and then looked at me, "Anything for you, Shae."

Later, as we ate, Shukree excitedly told me about the

agents that had been watching him. The NBA looked like a real possibility for him.

I lifted my fork up and examined the food on it before putting it in my mouth. "So, what are you going to do about all those groupies when you get to the NBA?"

Shrugging his shoulders, Shukree looked down at his plate. "The same thing I do now."

Sitting back in my chair, I put my fork down and folded my hands in my lap. "Seriously...you think I don't know what you do with them now?"

Shukree looked around, and then back at me, "With who? You've 'NEVER' seen me with anybody else, Shae."

Leaning over my plate, I looked at him until he looked up at me. "I'm sorry. I just want to make sure I understand what you're saying. Because I haven't 'SEEN' you with anyone else that means you haven't actually been with anyone else. That's what you're saying; right?" Shaking my head, I spoke barely above a whisper.

Shukree put his fork down and sat back in his chair with his arms folded across his chest. Silently, his eyes scanned my face.

Leaning over my plate, I continued to whisper, "I'm not trying to start an argument. Really, I'm not. But, for real, you think I don't know that you have sex with other people?"

"Where is this coming from, Shae, Melodi? What did she tell you?"

"Let me start over. Have you had sex with other girls since we've been together? And I'm not going to be mad, no matter what the answer is. Seriously, I won't be, because we don't have sex. I get it! I also get that you are a star on campus and I know what that means. So don't insult my intelligence by saying you're going to do the same thing in the NBA that you do in college."

Shukree slid further down in his chair. "You finished?"

I sat silently.

"Okay, here we go. You know I love you, Shae."

"Uh, huh…"

"Can I finish?"

"Uh, huh…"

"Like I said, I love you and of course I would never do anything to hurt you." Shaking his head, he looked directly at me. "Yeah, I've kicked it with a couple of other honeys. Yeah, I have." He stopped and bit on his bottom lip.

"So, I'm your what?"

Shukree sat up in his chair and put both of his hands up on the table. "Shae, don't do that. It's not like that."

I closed my eyes and shook my head. "You know what? I apologize. This whole conversation was uncalled for. I don't even know why I'm trippin' like this." I reached across the table and put my hand on top of one of his. "Okay, let's forget this whole conversation ever happened. You should be focused on your game and the agents in the bleachers, and the big ole' NBA." I flashed a smile as a peace offering. "First, and last, let me assure you, I am not mad. I'm not, Shukree. It is what it is and I know you care about me. I'm going to leave it at that."

Grabbing both of my hands and cupping them in between his, again, his eyes scanned my face. "Since we're sharing, have you been with anyone else, Shae?"

Smiling, I shook my head, "Of course not."

As Shukree kissed my hands, all I could think about was Shiloh.

TWENTY-THREE

I sat on the porch with Miss Alaina, preparing for her to smoke while we waited for Miss Zora to call us to breakfast, but she never lit anything.

"You feeling okay this morning, Miss Alaina?"

"Yes, why do you ask?"

I held my two fingers up to my lips and inhaled.

Ms. Alaina rocked forward as she laughed. "Oh, that. Yes, I'm fine. I need to, uhm..." She put her hand up to her mouth, as if in thought. "You know, Sister hasn't quite been herself and I need a clear head, so that I can pay closer attention to her."

"What do you mean?"

"Well, Sister and I don't know. We're just watching Sister a little closer these days. I'm sure it's nothing, though. Anyway...so congratulations again on your project and your class. We are all very pleased that you allowed us to play such a significant role in your education."

"I know I've thanked y'all over and over again, but I really can't thank you enough. I don't think I mentioned that I received the highest grade in the class. The professor said he wanted to talk with me about something in a few weeks, after I've had a little more time to settle into the new semester. I'm not sure what that's about, though."

"Maybe he's going to ask you to be his TA after you graduate in December. I wouldn't be surprised at all." She paused and looked out at the backyard. "When was the last time you talked with Shiloh?"

"I haven't. Not since the picnic."

Ms. Alaina turned and looked at me. "Are you serious? You don't have his phone number?"

I shook my head.

"Girl, you really are green. I suppose he doesn't have yours either."

"Nope..."

Laughing, she turned her attention back to the yard. "You know, you're still a little pitiful. You like him don't you?"

"Yes, ma'am, I do."

"Well, I see you learned one thing from me over the summer. You stopped with all that 'I don't know what you're talking about, Miss Alaina; who me, Miss Alaina?'" She laughed so hard she began coughing.

I handed her the glass of water that was on the end table next to her. After taking a sip she placed the glass back on the table. "Oooh, that was funny. Wasn't it, Miss Shae?"

I smiled. "Yes, it was. You know what else? Shukree and I broke up this week."

Her laughing stopped and she turned to look at me once again. "I'm really sorry to hear that."

"Are you really?" Though I, somehow, did not believe her, I smiled.

"No, really, I mean, I did want you two to break up. Actually, I thought you could date him and Shiloh at the same time, but I certainly didn't want you to be in a situation where you were hurt or, worse yet, alone. You broke up with Shukree, but you aren't with Shiloh either. That was not the master plan. What happened, if you don't mind me asking?"

"You know what? It wasn't even that big of a deal. We had a conversation early in the week – agents are really checking him out and he has a chance to get drafted into the NBA. For me, everything about our relationship finally hit home, and I had to ask myself if I really wanted to settle for what I had been settling for in school. You know, all of the other girls. He and I both knew where things were headed. The funny thing is, I'm not even mad about it. He's a pretty good guy, except for the other girls. I'm sure in time we would have gotten passed all of the groupies and the other women. What's really a trip, though, is he accused me of wanting to breakup because he thinks I like Shiloh."

Miss Alaina placed her hand on top of my hand, which was resting on my knee. "He's right. You do like Shiloh and Shiloh likes you. Not only that, he respects you too. Shukree 'thought' he was respecting you because he made all of the other girls stay away from you, but you and I both know that's not respect. That's something else. I ought to know." She paused and mischievously grinned. "Respect is when you're the only one, when he knows how to have self-control, how to be monogamous. I suppose that's what I wanted with Gollie." Her mind seemed to drift for just a few seconds. "Shiloh didn't have to introduce you to his girlfriend, but he did and, other than the occasional kiss...all you two did was kiss, right?"

Without thinking, I quickly snatched my hand up and gave her a playful smack on top of her hand as she continued to rest it on my knee. "Miss Alaina, you know that's all that happened."

"I don't know anything." Laughing, she playful grabbed her hand and feigned pain. "Like I was saying before you assaulted me, he didn't have to introduce the two of you. He was drawing the proverbial line in the sand, and he never really crossed it. A kiss or two, that's nothing. One of you needs to make a move, a real move, and it is okay if it's you. I mean, you just have to tell him how you feel. If it were me...well, I don't have to tell you what would happen if it were me. As a matter of fact, he would have known my intentions long before now." She paused and looked at me. "You should call him while you're here. Better yet, I'll call his family after breakfast to find out if he's in town and I'll get his phone number at Alabama State."

Before I could respond, Miss Zora appeared at the screen door. "Breakfast is ready. You two need to hurry before the food gets cold."

I turned and looked at Miss Zora as Miss Alaina used my knee as support to stand up.

"Don't let anybody tell you getting old is easy." She smiled. "Mother used to say that."

I stood up to follow her into the kitchen.

Stopping in the doorway, she turned and looked back at me. "Know what else Mother used to say?"

I shook my head.

"She used to say, 'Like the one that likes you.'"

TWENTY-FOUR

"Cheese grits, shrimp, scrambled eggs, and biscuits have never tasted so good, Miss Zora. I hope I can cook like this one day."

As she stood to clear the table, she smiled. "Well, I tell you, you don't have to go to school to cook grits. Please tell me you can cook grits."

The room filled with laughter.

"Yes, Miss Zora, I can cook grits, but there's no reason to as long as I can come here and eat them. As many times as I've cooked them, they've never tasted this good. I know you have some kind of secret."

She continued to smile as she raised her eyebrows and turned to walk to the kitchen.

Miss Claudette stood to help with the dishes, in spite of the fact that we all knew Ms. Zora always insisted on clearing the table herself. As she took the butter dish and the jelly off of the table, she looked over at me.

"Guess who I saw in town yesterday?"

Miss Alaina turned her glass up to get the last corner of mango juice that had earlier evaded her sip. Sitting the glass back on the table, she seemed to swish the juice around in her mouth.

"I don't know, who?"

"It was Shiloh. He's such a sweet young man. Apparently he's getting married next summer…"

Miss Alaina coughed and juice spewed across the table.

"Sister, are you okay?"

Holding one hand up and using the other to hold her chest, she continued to cough. "Excuse me? Are you sure you heard him correctly?"

Miss Claudette nodded her head. "Oh, absolutely, his mother was so excited she couldn't wait to tell me her baby boy was getting married." Turning back around, she whispered, "Milk…that's Sister's secret." She chuckled to herself as she exited the room, unaware of the effect of her unsettling announcement.

Miss Alaina and I turned and looked at each other. My eyes betrayed me as they surprisingly began to fill with tears.

"Miss Shae, I'm going to get up and call Shiloh's mother right now," Miss Alaina hurriedly whispered, as she looked over at the kitchen to make sure she hadn't been overheard."

"No, ma'am, please don't." I quickly jumped to my feet. "Don't…I mean…just don't."

"Shae…"

"No, I'm fine. Let me just get myself together." I

177

excused myself and quickly went upstairs to the bathroom.

I sat on the side of the bathtub as tears involuntarily pried their way through my closed eyes. I couldn't believe I was crying and over what? Shiloh and I were nothing to each other. So what, we liked each other and we kissed a couple of times. We never even talked about getting together, so why was I trippin'? So, okay, he's getting married. Shaking my head, I thought, *okay, makes sense now. That's why we haven't talked and, of course, because I never gave him my phone number. I can't believe this.* Shaking my head again, I stood up and turned the knob over the sink and splashed my face with some cold water. It is what it is. It's cool, though.

I dried my face with my towel and looked at the mirror. I had cried my mascara and eyeliner off, so my face looked naked. Before going downstairs, I went into what was now commonly referred to as my bedroom and did a little something to my eyes. I took one last look in the mirror before going back downstairs. I started laughing because I couldn't believe that I had just cried over a guy, a guy that wasn't even mine. I wondered what Miss Alaina's mother would have said about that.

I found all three sisters sitting in the parlor. They all stopped talking and looked at me as I entered the room.

Miss Zora stood up and walked over to me. "The food didn't make you sick did it, dear?"

Miss Alaina's eyes followed me as I took the few

steps across the room.

"Oh, no, ma'am, I'm fine. Sometimes you just have to, you know…" I smiled as I sat down. I was too embarrassed to explain anything.

"Okay, I just wanted to make sure. My cooking has never made anyone ill. Not as far as I know, so I was very concerned." Miss Zora sat back down in her seat. Immediately she became involved with something in her pocket.

Miss Claudette loudly slapped her knees with her hands. "Well, I think we should go for a ride to Birmingham. I feel like a day trip. We can do a little shopping and then maybe have lunch in town, as well. What do you think, Sister?

Miss Zora looked up at her then around the room at me and Miss Alaina. "Well, you know I prefer to eat my own cooking, but I think I can make an exception today, if Miss Shae agrees to do the driving."

"Of course, it would be my pleasure."

Miss Alaina stood up from her seat. "Well, if that's the case, I think we should go get ready, so that we can be chauffeured through town." She winked her eye at me as she left the room.

Our trip to Birmingham was pretty uneventful, except for when Miss Zora got lost. Fortunately, we had gone to an outlet mall and we didn't have to go running up and down the escalators to find her. Well, I didn't have to go running up and down the escalators. I asked Miss

Alaina to drive the car around the parking lot while I ran to each store and looked inside. It never occurred to us to check Kitchen Collection first, a store that sold anything you could ever want for your kitchen, but it made perfectly good sense that we would find Miss Zora there. She was not lost, we were.

On the ride back to Jemison, Miss Alaina sat in the front seat with me. The ride home was quiet, except for the music that played on the radio and the heavy breathing of Miss Claudette and Miss Zora after they dozed off.

After about 15 minutes, Miss Alaina turned to look at her sisters as they napped in the backseat. "Are you okay? This morning, Sister's news took me by surprise too. That was the last thing I was expecting to hear," she whispered.

I glanced over at her, but quickly turned my attention back to the road.

"Have you reverted back to being coy? What are we going to do about Shiloh?"

"What do you mean?"

"He's not married yet"

"So you're suggesting I be the other woman. If that's what you're saying, I can tell you that's not going to happen. As a matter of fact, I'm not going to do anything. He's engaged to be married! I don't want to be the person that interferes with that."

Miss Alaina glanced over her shoulder at the backseat again. "Shhh...you don't have to raise your voice."

"Sorry, I didn't mean to get loud, but really, Miss Alaina? His family is planning a wedding and then here I come telling him, 'Oh, I meant to tell you, I really like you. Can we date before you get married?'"

"Look here, let me tell you something. Today we heard he's getting married 'next summer.' I repeat, 'next summer.' Anything, I mean, anything can happen between now and then. You don't know what all of this really means. Did he ask her to marry him or did he just tell his parents that he was going to ask her to marry him? All I know is he's not ready to get married. He just kissed you over the summer…twice! Is that a man that's ready to get married? He's a good boy. He likes you, Shae. Like him back and see where it goes."

"But I don't want to get hurt, Miss Alaina." I quickly turned and looked at her.

"But if you don't say anything neither one of you will ever know and you'll spend the rest of your life wondering what could have been. I can still call his family when we get back to the house." Pointing at the back seat, "When we get home, those two are still going to be sleepy. I can make that call while they finish their naps. They'll never have to know."

I stared straight ahead at the road as she spoke. Before leaving the house for Birmingham, I had already come to the conclusion that I had lost my opportunity to get to know Shiloh. If the shoe were on the other foot and I was the one getting married, I would be pretty pissed off if someone came to me talkin' about they 'like' me, like that's supposed to make me break off my engagement. The decision had been made and that was that.

"I'm not worried about Miss Claudette and Miss Zora. I don't want to bother Shiloh. I had my chance and I blew it, so I would sincerely appreciate it if you just, kind of, leave it alone. Please don't call him or his family. I would hate for his mom and dad to treat me like your Gollie's parents treated you. That would be worse then what's happening now."

"Touché, you win. I got it. Even though I didn't share information about my life with you for you to use it against me, you made your point." Miss Alaina closed her eyes and lie back on her seat.

The rest of the ride to Jemison was filled with silence, except for the soft music that played on the radio.

TWENTY-FIVE

It wasn't until I went to visit my family for the fall break that I realized that I had only seen Shukree play basketball a handful of times after we started dating. My brother asked about his stats and I was embarrassed that I couldn't answer any of his questions. I guess it played right into Shukree's hands. It allowed him to date as many girls as he wanted. It also showed how much I really wasn't into him. That's crazy when you think about it. Melodi and I talked about everything, but we've never talked about that. She went to all of the games and she always invited me to go, and I always said no. I said it was because I didn't want to 'distract' him.

While I was home, I learned that my mom and dad were happy that I had become close friends with the Roberts sisters. They had talked with them on the phone several times and had made plans to go visit them in December during my winter break, to my younger siblings' disappointment. I was excited to share my family with three women who had become my new family, my aunts, and equally as excited to share the Roberts sisters with my actual family.

Time seemed to fly. I was busy trying to get the highest GPA that I could possibly get to go on to graduate school. Melodi was doing the same, in addition to still partying because it was our last semester at Miles. In spite of being roommates, we hadn't being seeing much of each other. One more month, though, and we would be college graduates.

I always received calls from Ms. Alaina or Miss Claudette, but there's one call that I received from Miss Claudette that I will never forget. I wasn't particularly busy. It was just a normal morning. I was supposed to be getting ready for class. The phone didn't seem to ring any differently than it had any other time, but the first thing I heard when I put the receiver to my ear was the sound of muffled sobs in the background. As soon as Miss Claudette spoke, I knew something was wrong. She explained to me that they had lost Sister that morning. I quickly realized the sobbing was Miss Alaina.

Miss Zora had been officially diagnosed with Alzheimer's just a few months earlier. After her diagnosis, I began to visit every weekend to help Miss Claudette and Miss Alaina. I knew that it was going to be difficult for them to see their older sister progressively reduced to a fraction of herself; silent and helpless, eventually becoming almost like a baby. They had told me about her diagnosis over the phone, but when I was there we never spoke of it. As a matter of fact, we never talked about it again. I usually helped clean the house, wash the clothes and linen, and on rare occasion made tea. I also assisted them when they took Miss Zora to sit on the back porch to get a little fresh air. We did this until she forgot how to walk. After that they made sure the curtains of her bedroom window were open, so that the sun could always shine into the room.

Every day Miss Claudette dutifully sat next to her sister's bed and either read to her or talked with her – whether or not Miss Zora was awake. When Miss Claudette had to take a break, Miss Alaina took over, but there was very little of that 'wild crazy' talk, as Miss Zora had often referred to it, that Miss Alaina was so fondly known for. She was merely Miss Zora's little sister again. She often talked about times when they were children or about their mother and father. She laughed a lot when she talked with her big sister. Sometimes she whispered in her ear, about what I have no idea. Miss Alaina had also taken over the responsibility of cooking. Before Miss Zora stopped cooking, I never knew that Miss Alaina was such a good cook. She said she had been taught by the best, her big sister.

After receiving the call, I called my mom and dad and told them what had happened and that I was going to miss the next few days, or more, of school because I was going to Jemison to be with Miss Claudette and Miss Alaina. I also contacted my professors and told them that one of my great-aunts had died. By now, Shukree and I were no longer speaking, so I left a note in the apartment for Melodi, to let her know that I would be in Jemison, but that I would call her with the details once the arrangements had been made. It was difficult to pack my suitcase through my tears. Miss Zora and I had grown as close as I think we possibly could, under the circumstances.

As I sped down the highway to Jemison, my mind also raced through some of the memories of the past few months, like when Miss Zora confided in me that she had been forgetting things and had to resort to writing little notes so that she could remember what she was supposed to do or even how to cook. She even told me how she had been going to specialists and that they thought it was either the early onset of dementia or, worse yet, Alzheimer's. I think she told me before she even told her sisters. She was scared. She didn't want to forget the things that were important to her: her sisters, her life in Paris, her late husband Hervey Thériault, her son Patric Olivier, or how to cook. She didn't want to forget me either. One day, she even told me about how she met her husband and fell in love with him and how before giving birth to her son she had no idea that she could love another human being so much. She told me to have babies, as many as I could, because it would bring an unimaginable joy to my life.

Before things took a turn for the worse, there was one day when I was visiting the sisters, early in the day, Miss Zora called me into the kitchen. I couldn't imagine that she was going to ask me to help her cook because she never wanted assistance in the kitchen, even then. When I walked into the room I merely said yes, ma'am.

Miss Zora turned around and handed me a small mason jar of fruit. "When you first started visiting us, I never gave you anything but a hard time. Please accept this from me as a gift. I never meant to be so harsh with you. Initially, I resented you, but I have grown very fond of you and your presence in our home. I've come to look forward to not only your visits and cooking meals for you but the youthful energy and excitement you bring to our lives. You have so much of your life in front of you – 'LIVE IT!' My life has been wonderful. I know the best of it is now behind me. Please accept this very small token from me and promise me...you...will live...your life...to the fullest!"

I nodded my head to keep from crying. She was pleased, so she turned away from me and again focused her attention on preparing a meal. Not even ten minutes after leaving the kitchen, we smelled something burning. When we rushed in to see what was going on, Miss Zora was standing in the middle of the kitchen confused. She had no idea what she was doing. Miss Claudette, Miss Alaina, and I cleaned up the mess she had made. When I finished, I walked over to her as she sat in a chair watching us. I asked what she wanted me to do next. She reached up and gently placed her hands on either side of my face and thanked me, but when I looked in her eyes they were empty. Immediately, I knew that she no longer recognized me. I asked if she knew my name. She nodded and said yes, but she never said my name again. I could feel the tears involuntarily streaming down my cheeks as Miss Alaina grasped my hand and guided me to the back porch and held me as I cried uncontrollably.

TWENTY-SIX

If there was such a thing as a beautiful day for a funeral,
today would have been the day. I don't think the weather
could have been any more pleasant or the sky any bluer.
I don't even think there could have been a gentler breeze
blowing. I couldn't stop looking up at the clouds that
filled the sky like white, fluffy marshmallows. A few
times, I know I smiled to myself as tears slowly
cascaded down my cheeks and fell to the green grass
below. I caught others glancing at me. I smiled at them
through my tears. They probably thought I was crazy,
but I knew Miss Zora would have been pleased with
everything: the service, how regal, composed, and
genteel her sisters were, especially how well-behaved
Miss Alaina was; the music that seemed to serenade the
air in an attempt to distract us from our sadness; the food
that was served – she would have only been more
pleased with this if she herself had prepared and served
it, and she would have been very pleased with how

beautiful the day had been for her funeral.

It seemed like the entire town attended the services, including Shiloh and his family. He and I hadn't talked since the picnic the year before, so I avoided him. It wasn't difficult because there were so many people. My parents couldn't come, but they spoke with Miss Claudette and Miss Alaina and they sent a beautiful flower arrangement. I hadn't noticed at the funeral because I sat on the front pew with Miss Claudette and Miss Alaina, but when I went back to the Roberts sisters' home I ran into Melodi. It was good to see her.

We hugged each other so hard that I thought we would both lose our breath.

"Are you okay, Shae?"

I nodded my head. "Yeah, have Miss Claudette and Miss Alaina seen you?"

"Yes, they saw me at the graveside."

We held hands as we walked across the backyard toward the house.

"Okay, that's good. I think I'm going to stay for at least a couple more days to help clean up and, you know. So I won't be able to take you back to Miles, unless you want to stay too?"

Melodi looked away at the house. "I'm good."

"How did you get here anyway?"

She shrugged her shoulders. As we walked hand in hand, Shukree came through the gate. As he got closer, he reached out for me, so I released Melodi's hand.

"Thank you for coming, Shukree. That was really nice of you."

"They welcomed me to their home last summer and I know Miss Zora and both of her sisters mean a lot to you." He continued to hug me as he spoke. He was always a good hugger. Eventually he released me and stepped back. "Melodi, we have to leave soon because I have to get back for a meeting with Coach."

"Oh, y'all rode together…wait, y'all rode together?"

Shukree was now standing next to Melodi as she continued to look anywhere but at me.

"Melodi, are you and Shukree…nah, don't tell me you and Shukree are, like, together. Seriously, Shukree, you're dating Melodi?"

He looked down at Melodi then at me. "I thought you knew. Melodi, you didn't tell Shae we were together?"

Doe-eyed, Melodi looked at me for the first time since Shukree had set foot in the backyard. "Shae, it's not like we planned it or anything. It just happened. I was hanging out with the team after a game. We started talking…and, you know. I'm sorry."

"And here I was thinking we were missing each other because we were both so busy trying to make sure we graduated." Pausing, I turned and looked away for a moment to gather my thoughts. "You know what? I'm not mad. I'm disappointed, but I'm not mad. But you know, you're supposed to be my friend, so you should have come to me…"

"I didn't need your permission, Shae."

"I wasn't going to say that. What I was going to say was, you should have come to me and told me what was up. That's what friends do. I can't say what would have happened, but I know it wouldn't have been like me, you, and Shukree would have been hanging out together after that. You should have said something. He was my boyfriend."

"Y'all weren't together anymore and it just happened. So, I'm supposed to come to you and say the dude that you had been dating and that I couldn't stand was now my boyfriend? I was too embarrassed." She stopped and looked up at Shukree, "No, disrespect, baby."

Shukree grasped her hand, "It's cool."

I looked at both of them and I wanted to be mad. I think I was a little, but I was too sad about Miss Zora to be mad, though. Friends don't do friends like that. You don't date your best friend's ex-boyfriend. Do you? I'm sure when I tell Miss Alaina about them she'll ask me why I even care. I'm sure she had, at some point in her life, been in the same position as Melodi.

I looked up at Shukree then down at Melodi. "You know what? See y'all later." I turned and walked through the crowd towards the path that led to the water porch.

I wasn't surprised to find people sitting out there because people were everywhere, so I went to the water's edge and sat down to look at the water.

"You want to be alone or can I sit with you?"

I turned and looked up. It was Shiloh. I shook my head in disbelief because I had been coming to Jemison regularly and had not seen him in months, and now he seemed to appear out of nowhere.

"Oh, was that a no?"

"No, you can sit." I looked out at the water then at him after he sat down. "So you're following people now?"

"I guess I am."

He sat uncomfortably close to me.

"I'm sorry about Miss Zora."

"I should say the same to you. You've known her all your life."

"Yeah, I was surprised when I heard she had died. I was more surprised when I first heard she had Alzheimer's, though. That was crazy."

"Yeah, it was. I came down every weekend to help out as much as I could. It was horrible seeing her like that. And as horrible as it was for me, I can only imagine how Miss Claudette and Miss Alaina must have felt."

"Yeah, I came by to see them a few times. I didn't want to see Miss Zora because one of my grandmothers had Alzheimer's. I just didn't want to see her like that."

"They never mentioned that you came by."

"I asked them about you."

My head snapped around and I looked at him. "Oh, yeah? They never mentioned it."

"I guess they had other things on their minds."

"You're probably right." I closed my eyes for just a second then continued. "Why would you be asking about me?" I turned my attention back to the water and a little twig I had picked up off the ground. "Your wedding date should be coming up in a couple of months or so, huh?"

"Yeah..." He nodded his head but focused his

attention on the water as he spoke.

"Shiloh…"

"Yeah?"

There was nothing to say. As I stood up, I brushed debris from my dress and slipped my feet back into my shoes. "This isn't even a conversation that we're going to have. You could have gotten in touch with me if you really wanted to."

He grabbed my hand as I turned to walk away. "You could have gotten in touch with me too, Shae."

I looked down at our hands and pulled away from him. "I suppose there were a lot of things we could have done, but we didn't. And you know what? It really doesn't matter now."

He stood up, so we silently began to walk until we reached the path. Then we silently walked the path until we reached the tree line, where we both stopped and gazed at the crowd that was still gathered in the backyard.

Turning to look at him, I raised my eyebrows and extended my arms. "I never congratulated you."

We hugged each other hard then we both took a step back.

"Thanks, Shae."

I began to walk towards the house as he walked towards his family that was standing not too far away.

TWENTY-SEVEN

"This venture in my life started off as a class project, which led me to a book written by Miss Claudette Roberts, 'The Emancipation Continuum of the Negro in America.' I had no idea that it would take me on an adventure of a lifetime, and in such a short amount of time. Nor did I know that it would allow me the pleasure of getting acquainted with three magnificently 'brilliant' women, Miss Claudette Roberts and her sisters, Miss Zora Roberts and Miss Alaina Roberts, who together lived through times of historical significance for Black Americans, and who individually had experiences that we only read about in books. I can honestly say meeting them has thus far been one of the most enlightening and gratifying times in my life.

What I thought I knew about myself, including my history as a black woman, was completely altered after I met them. They shared information with me that led me to understand that I have a responsibility, not just to myself, but to those that came before me, whose strength and perseverance is what even allows me to exist.

In addition to that, each one of them taught me something different. Miss Claudette taught me to take my life and my responsibilities seriously because there is a debt owed for the privileges that I have. Miss Zora taught me to be unafraid of opening my heart to love and to try to love beyond whatever tragedies may occur in my life. Miss Alaina, well, where should I begin?" Smiling, I turned and looked at her. "First of all, there are some things that she taught me that I cannot mention here today."

The room erupted in laughter along with me.

"If you ever have the pleasure of talking with her or spending any amount of time with her, you will immediately understand what I mean, but, seriously, she taught me about taking chances as a young woman and understanding that life right now is not finite, and that this moment in time does not necessarily determine who I am or what I will do with my life. At that moment, it's still all yet to be determined, but I should pay close attention to those moments and consciously or subconsciously consider them in the whole of my life as I plan my next steps, my next experience, or what have you. Along with her sisters, she also taught me that life is an adventure and that I should live it, that I should take advantage of every moment as an opportunity to be educated or to educate others, to not allow anything to surprise me, and to never hold grudges.

So, when Professor Snead approached me in my last

semester at Miles College and suggested I expand the class project he had assigned in the previous semester into a book, I was shocked because I had never considered anything like that. I merely wanted an 'A' on the project and an 'A' in his class." Laughing, I turned and looked at Professor Snead proudly sitting in the front row. "He explained that he had shared my completed project with an editor friend of his and that this friend showed immediate interest after reading it because, in his words, 'My friend was as equally moved by your writing as I had been when I read it.' He said he looked forward to discussions of the status of my project each week and that his anticipation to read the completed project often overwhelmed him, and that it did not leave him disappointed when he received it.

So, to Professor Snead, thank you for opening a door for me, and I thank the Roberts sisters for unknowingly teaching me that I had to walk through the door to experience the next adventure in my life. Oh, yes, and I thank my parents for their patience, understanding, and concern about me driving to Jemison by myself to meet strangers, who turned out to be outstanding mentors and friends."

Teary-eyed, I held up my book and looked over at Miss Claudette and Miss Alaina. "I really wish Miss Zora could have been here because I know she would have been proud of me, even if she never said it. Better yet, I know she would have been overjoyed by either cooking a meal for me tonight or by catering this event because whenever she cooked it was extremely apparent that love was the foremost ingredient of each one of her recipes. So, because of that, I not only dedicate this book, 'Yet to be Determined,' to you, the Roberts sisters, for providing the real substance of the book, but especially to Miss Zora, who taught me to always make love the most important ingredient. Thank you."

ABOUT THE AUTHOR

T.R. Baker is a judicial assistant for a DeKalb County, Georgia, State Court judge. *Yet to be Determined* is her third novel. Her debut novel, *Every Time I Close My Eyes*, was originally published in 2003, and then re-released in March 2013. Her second novel, *Daddy's Big Girl*, was published in 2014.

Follow the author at:

www.simplytrbaker.com

www.simplytrb.blogspot.com

www.facebook.com/tayarbaker2

https://twitter.com/Simplytrbaker

Email the author at:

www.simplytrbaker@gmail.com